Like a wasp, I was hatched into fury
The world was a razorblade
If I clearly was so early done for
For what was I ever made?

—The Dogs, *G.U.I.L.T.Y.*

THE

NIHILIST

A NOVEL

KEIJO KANGUR

THE NIHILIST
A Novel

Second Edition

First published in 2020

Copyright © 2021, 2020 Keijo Kangur

This is a work of fiction. However, some of the
characters, places and incidents are based on real
life. Names have been changed. Any resemblance
to actual persons should be apparent to them. The
opinions expressed are those of the character and
may or may not belong to the author.

Editing by Maria Sütt
Book design by Keijo Kangur
Cover photography by Maria Sütt

ISBN: 979-8-6632-1634-0

www.keijokangur.com

Nihilism is the belief that all values are baseless and that nothing can be known or communicated. It is often associated with extreme pessimism and a radical skepticism that condemns existence. A true nihilist would believe in nothing, have no loyalties, and no purpose other than, perhaps, an impulse to destroy.[*]

---

[*] "Nihilism," by Alan Pratt, The Internet Encyclopedia of Philosophy, www.iep.utm.edu

1

A WOMAN WITH BLACK hair and painted lips pointed a revolver at my face and pulled the trigger. When the bullet exited the barrel of the gun, however, everything went into super slow motion, and I could see as the projectile slowly traveled towards my forehead.

Eventually, after it had penetrated my skull and entered my brain, I could feel my consciousness starting to fade away and with it the whole world began falling away, piece by piece, like a house of cards, as I slowly succumbed into nothingness. And as I did, I felt the greatest sense of peace that I had ever felt in my life.

After I woke up from my dream, I realized that I didn't want to be awake at all. I wanted the dream to continue. Forever. For being dead didn't hurt. Only being alive did.

Most people feared death and the nothingness it brought. That's why we had invented impossible ideas such as rebirth and afterlife, why we put dying people on life support, why suicide was stigmatized, and why we in general tried to think about death as little as possible.

Yet there was nothing wrong with being dead. No one that was dead wanted to be alive. And no one that was unborn wanted to be born. Those of us that were alive only had a vested interest in existence because we already existed. The dead did not share our passion.

Although it was thought that death was something strange, that it was unnatural, that it was something to be abolished, it was obvious that death was in fact the standard in the universe. Surrounded by infinite nothingness on both sides, it was life that was the great exception.

The living being, as Nietzsche said, was ultimately only a species of the dead. And a very rare species at that.

2

AFTER ABOUT AN HOUR of lying in bed, thinking about the dream I'd had, I finally forced myself up and got dressed. I was at an all-time low. It was Saturday.

I went to the fridge and grabbed a slice of cold pepperoni pizza that I had ordered the day before. Sitting on the couch of my small living room/kitchen, I ate the pizza whilst gazing outside into the distance through the black venetian blinds. It looked gloomy out there. Autumn had arrived just in time.

I'd had hope once . . . but my hope had all but vanished by now. Hope was a finite resource. It needed to be constantly replenished. By money. By love. By a success—or illusion—of some sort. And I had none. I was working at a job I despised, barely making enough to survive. My girlfriend of three years had recently left me. I had no friends. And, although I wanted to be a writer, I couldn't write.

All in all, I felt as though I was in a hole and the hole was so deep that the only thing left to do was to keep on digging until I could feel the flames of hell underneath my feet.

And why not? Everything just kept on repeating anyway. We woke up. We went to work. We ate. We slept. We suffered through misery. We kept our brains satiated with meaningless entertainment or alcohol in order to dull the misery of our routine. And yet, although we hated our routine, we couldn't imagine life without it. We were slaves to it. This was our paradox. And I was no exception.

Vicky leaving me had shattered my routine. I had come to rely on her. I had needed her. And then all of a sudden, she was gone. And I was alone. Alone in the entire universe. Or so it seemed. Naturally, I had considered suicide. But I was weak. I feared pain. If only there was a painless way to do it . . . but there wasn't. As far as I knew.

I glanced at my surroundings. My apartment was a fucking pigsty. Empty boxes of pizza and Chinese food littered the room, along with countless empty bottles of beer, whiskey, and wine. My diet had been lousy for a while now. It would end up killing me eventually. Unless I killed myself first.

After I was done with the pizza, I walked to the sink to get a glass of water. The sink was full of dirty dishes. It reminded me of the kitchen sink in the movie *Withnail and I.* Unspeakable things were floating in it, potentially alive. I hadn't washed the dishes in weeks because I hated washing dishes. In fact, I hated all menial chores. And life, as far as I was concerned, was full of menial chores. It felt strange how we had to do so many pointless little things over and over again just to be alive when being alive wasn't even all that good.

Still, as I was planning to go out—for you see, I couldn't stay in this tomb of an apartment for too long all by myself in fear of going crazy—I decided to freshen myself up a bit. So I took a shower, trimmed my beard, slicked my hair back with gel, and picked out a nice black shirt to wear, the only one I got. When I was all done, I went to the mirror and looked at my reflection. I looked like a man going to his own funeral.

At first after Vicky had left me, I had gotten drunk at home. I had passed the time by listening to melancholic rock songs, masturbating, practicing five finger fillet and slowly going insane. All very healthy habits, I know.

However, the atmosphere in the apartment soon became unbearable to me as I continued seeing her shadow in every corner. And so, I started going out to bars instead, where I drank myself into oblivion whilst trying to have meaningful conversations with random strangers. A futile endeavor as ever.

It wasn't so much that I was searching for something, but rather that I was trying to get away from her shadow.

And, perhaps, also from my own.

3

WHEN I STEPPED OUT of the apartment, I noticed that a note had been crudely stuck through my front door handle. I picked it up. From its poor grammar, it looked like it had been written by a Russian.

I read the note whilst walking down the stairs. "Stop listening to music so loudly at night," it said. "People are trying to sleep. If you want to listen to music at night, use headphones. Otherwise, we will call the police. Or you will be evicted."

What the note said was indeed true. But then music—at least the kind I listened to—was *meant* to be listened to loudly and at odd hours. And I couldn't stand wearing headphones. To me, music was like water. It needed to fill the room. So that I could drown in it. Besides, they had no idea what I was going through. So fuck 'em, I thought, as I crumpled the note and threw it away.

Outside, I walked to a small store nearby in order to buy some cigarettes. It was a Russian-owned store where time stood still. I didn't like going there since the cashiers only spoke in Russian and all the food they sold was close to the expiration date. But since it was the nearest shop to my apartment and they sold some cheap—and strong—Russian beer there, I often frequented it.

As usual when I stepped into the store there were no people around aside from a couple of cashiers and a security guard. I often wondered how the store was able to remain in operation. Perhaps it was a front for money laundering?

After I got my Marlboro Reds and exited the store, I lit a cigarette and walked to the bus stop at the nearby plaza, which was surrounded by a casino, a liquor store, a sleazy bar, and a pawnshop. All of the necessities of life were there.

Whilst waiting for the bus, I saw an old man uncork a bottle of vodka and take a hit from it. I didn't blame him. Life was hard. And sometimes you had to do anything you could just in order to survive. Even if others scorned you for it. But what did they know? Fuck 'em.

The bus arrived and I stepped on. As it started moving, I looked out the window at all the people passing by on the streets, wondering how they had all managed to live day by day in this crazy world for such a long time without having gone insane from the banality of everyday life—from its endless repetition, its constant disappointments, its inherent emptiness.

Then it hit me—they *were* insane. They had gone insane a long time ago. They *had* to in order to want to continue repeating the same inane bullshit every day—such as sitting in traffic, standing in lines, wrestling with bureaucracy, working at a lousy job with low pay, being looked down upon, getting brainwashed by advertising, getting fucked by the government, having a dysfunctional relationship, a stupid child, a decaying body, and so on.

They were all insane and I simply didn't have the good luck of having gone insane like they had.

I always did have such rotten luck.

4

AFTER I STEPPED OFF the bus in the city center, I headed towards a nearby Irish pub called Dublin. It was one of my usual places.

It was about three in the afternoon when I entered the pub. I ordered the strongest beer they had on tap and sat in a corner furnished with a worn mahogany table and chairs, as well as a dark green leather bench. On the walls were portraits of random Irish celebrities, movie stars, and musicians, such as Enya, Gabriel Byrne, and the autistic girl from Harry Potter. I was certain they'd never been in the pub, so I wasn't sure of the reason for having their portraits on the walls, but I assumed it had something to do with celebrity worship.

I took a sip and looked around. A bunch of young women sat at a table nearby, talking enthusiastically about something. I couldn't hear them all that well, but they looked like students to me, so I imagined that they were talking about some event or party, no doubt connected to the college they were all attending.

I myself had never been to college. I had wanted to, but life had other things in mind. Perhaps things would have been better had I attended one. Then again, perhaps not. It was impossible to know for sure. Besides, I didn't really believe in free will, so what did it matter? As far as I was concerned, everything was inevitable. Every joy and every suffering. Every ill-treatment. Every humiliation. Every disappointment. Every fuck-up. Every bad experience. The world was painfully unfair to those who weren't lucky enough to have arrived at a better random, yet inevitable, outcome. In other words, to people like me.

But then, for so many people it was so much worse. After all, I wasn't starving. I wasn't being tortured. I didn't have any debilitating disease—aside from existence that is. And yet I suffered. Perhaps it was because I didn't have anything particular to suffer from that I suffered so deeply from the general misfortune of being alive. Would I have been happier if, for instance, I didn't have any legs?

After I had finished my beer and ordered another one, I took a book out of my coat pocket. It was *Will O' the Wisp* by Pierre Drieu la Rochelle. It was the first English print from 1966 and had cost almost eighty pounds.

I had brought this particular book with me because it was one of the most somber and hopeless books I had ever read. It thus went well with my present state of mind. The book told the story of Alain, a depressed heroin addict who was tired of living. And, despite not being a heroin addict myself—if only because I lacked access to it—I could easily identify with Alain's blight.

Indeed, I seemed to share his lethargy now more than ever.

I opened the first page and began reading:

At that moment, Alain was watching Lydia relentlessly. But he had been gazing at her like that ever since she arrived in Paris three days earlier. What was he waiting for? Sudden enlightenment about her or himself.

I read a few chapters before putting the book away. I could rarely read very much at once. Sooner or later, my mind began drifting off. With badly written books, this usually happened on the very first page. But then, most books weren't worth reading anyway; they were written only to make money.

I looked around. The girls nearby were gone. Other strangers had replaced them, all of them equally faceless. I wished there was someone to talk to. But this wasn't a good place to socialize with strangers.

I took out my phone and looked through my contacts. There weren't many. Of the few people with whom I'd once had some deeper connection, one was now living in another country, one was an ex-girlfriend who hated me, one was an ex who was indifferent towards me, and one was the ex who had recently left me, reducing me thereby to a state not unlike a glass balloon. I decided to go with the latter option.

I rang but she didn't pick up. I also sent her a text

message, though I doubted she'd be answering it any time soon because of her job. I didn't feel like contacting anyone else. I had alienated nearly everybody I had ever gotten to know, even the few people that I had actually liked. I wasn't sure why I had alienated the ones I had liked, but regarding the others the answer was simple. I simply didn't like them. Why? Because they weren't up to my standards.

In fact, one of the things that made everyday life so terrible for me was that on each day I usually had to come into contact with at least some of these so-called human beings. And every time I did, I was reminded all over again how ugly the world was. How it was populated with such ugly beings. Beings who thought that they were kings and queens, yet, as a famous singer once put it, they were all fucking peasants as far as I could see.

Ah, fuck it, I thought. I'd call an old friend of mine. He was always up for a beer or two. I didn't like him much, but beggars can't be choosers.

5

I WAS ON MY third beer when Martin stepped into the bar. He acknowledged me with a curt nod and went to order a beer at the counter.

I had known Martin for years. We had first met while working at the same data entry job at a company which by now had gone bankrupt. He was good for drinking with, but profound conversations weren't exactly his forte. Considering he studied law, that may not have been altogether surprising.

"So what's the occasion?" he asked, placing his beer down on my table.

"The occasion, my dear Martin, is that there is no occasion. For you see, all occasions are equally meaningless and made-up. Therefore, having no occasion to drink is not only *as* good an occasion for drinking as an actual 'occasion' but even better since we choose it ourselves instead of being led like sheep."

"Uh-huh," he said, seemingly not understanding what I was talking about.

I sighed. "Let's just say I wanted some company. And since I don't have any friends, I invited you."

He looked at me awkwardly and chuckled. "Oh come on now, I'm your friend."

But am I yours?

We sipped on our beers in silence for a while. I looked around. Much like a human body being taken over by cancer, the pub was slowly filling up with people.

"So how's life?" Martin finally asked.

Ah yes, the typical question.

"What do you think, Martin? It's shit. Just like it has always been. In fact, I'm thinking of hanging myself."

He chuckled. I had told so many suicide jokes to him over the years that he had long since stopped taking me seriously on them. I was like the boy who cried wolf. But at the same time, I was the wolf.

"And how's yours?" I asked.

"Oh, the usual."

"In other words, shit?"

"I wouldn't quite say that."

A pity. I wish you did.

We ordered another beer. We talked about life, work, our mutual acquaintances, and so on. As usual, Martin didn't seem to have anything very interesting to say. Finally unable to tolerate the dull conversation any longer, I suddenly asked him whether he believed in God.

"Well, uh, I'm not religious if that's what you mean. Not sure about God though."

"Did I ever tell you where religion and God came from?"

"Not that I recall, no."

"Well, then let me tell you." I took a big sip of beer and cleared my throat, trying to recall a few audio lectures I had heard on the topic some time ago.

"Thousands of years ago," I began, "there lived in a big castle a big guy called the king, who owned a lot of land and ruled over thousands of people who all lived in squalor and misery. And since they had nothing, they tended to steal from the only place there was anything worth stealing from, which was the king's castle. Now, naturally the king spent a fortune on hired guards, but they weren't doing a very good job and occasionally even stole from the king themselves.

"Then one day a wizard appeared before the king and claimed he could prevent the people from stealing from him without needing any guards. Greedy as the king was, he agreed to try the wizard's method. At first, the wizard caught the attention of the people by showing them a few magic tricks, much like magicians do nowadays, but which the primitive people took at face value. Then he told them that the being who granted him such powers lives high up in the sky and is called God. God is all-powerful and all-seeing, he said, and has sent *him* to tell *them* that they must always obey the king. They must always do what the king says and never steal from him. And if they don't, God's punishment will be severe. They will grow sick, their children will die, their fields will wither. And that's how the wizard made the people god-fearing—by scaring the shit out of them."

The pub was beginning to get quite crowded and noisy. "To enforce the word of God," I continued in a louder voice, "a large and powerful building was built, called the church, and the wizard became its priest. The church came with rules—no more stealing, no more killing, and no more fucking around. Because God said so.

"Well, these rules worked for a while, but eventually there was a famine and the people started stealing from the king again. So in order to appease them, the priest invited the people to the church and told them that they too would one day live in a big castle and have feasts beyond their wildest dreams, just like the king. And when the people asked him when, he said right after they die. Because that's when they go to heaven, where there is no work, no disease, no hunger, where everything is free, everyone is happy, everyone lives forever, and everyone is king.

"And this impressed the people so much that they started to believe in it, because in this way it seemed as though all their earthly toil and suffering was worth it in the end. And so they slaved and starved and suffered on and on and even went to war for the king, all in the name of a God created out of a thirst for power and embodied in fear and false promise. And the priest? He became rich and lived comfortably. Of course, after he died, his successors took his lies as truth and went on preaching them. And that, dear Martin, is essentially how religion and faith in God came to be."

Although Martin seemed to have been mesmerized by my story, as was to be expected, he still asked me how I knew that that's the way it happened.

"You mean how do I know that it's all a big fraud?"

"Well, yes."

"Because in the Bible it says that Moses cast a staff before the Pharaoh and the staff became a snake. But did you know that if you take a certain type of snake and squeeze an area behind its neck it becomes rigid like a stick?"

"Can't say I did, no."

"It also says that Moses put his staff into water and the water turned into blood. But do you think that *really* happened, or did he simply use a hollow bamboo tube with a red dye in it? Which one's more plausible?"

"The second option I guess."

"And then it says that Moses talked to God at the top of a mountain through a burning bush." I shook my head in disbelief. "Although I sincerely doubt that ever happened, for argument's sake, let's say it did."

"Okay."

"Well, first of all, when you spend a lot of time on top of a mountain, you can get oxygen-deprived, which leads to hallucinations, particularly the kind where you feel that someone you can't see is there with you. This has been confirmed by numerous mountain climbers. And secondly, if there was indeed a 'burning bush,' it was probably just a will-o'-the-wisp, a natural phenomenon in nature which happens through chemoluminescence.

"In other words, Moses was nothing more than a magician or a hallucinating fool. And in fact, there are people like him even today—magicians who think they have real magical powers, or at least they tell the public they do. Like the spoon-bending Uri Geller, for instance."

"Who's that?"

"Just another charlatan."

"What's that?"

"Never mind. However, I'm sure you've heard of the Virgin Mary statue in India which 'miraculously' wept?"

Martin thought for a moment. "Yeah, I vaguely recall hearing something about that."

"But did you know that when a skeptic investigated this, it turned out that the water dripping off the statue's face was caused by the broken plumbing of a nearby toilet? Which, of course, didn't stop thousands of Hindus from praying before it and kissing its dirty feet."

Martin squinted his eyes and tilted his head. "You're sure it came from the plumbing?"

"Yes, Martin, I'm sure. All so-called miracles are based on misunderstanding. Or they're just flat out lies. For instance, did you know that the flood myth in the Bible was plagiarized from *The Epic of Gilgamesh*?"

"What's that?"

"Mankind's oldest surviving literary work. Which, believe it or not, I've actually read."

"Was it any good?"

"No." I paused to take a sip of beer. "Of course, given that this is all ancient history, you can't really *prove* anything unless you use things like radiocarbon dating, which you obviously can't for the things I'm talking about. So you've got to ask yourself instead, what makes sense? I mean . . . how else do you think they controlled all those people? By deceiving them of course! That's what religion was designed for. It's the oldest scam in the book. The king had everything he wanted, you see, and he wanted to keep it that way. Which he did—through violence, manipulation and lies. And he was helped along by the priest."

Martin seemed indifferent. "If you say so."

"I do say so. I say that the first king was nothing but a gangster and the first priest a fucking phony. And as a philosopher once put it, man will never be free until the last king is strangled by the entrails of the last priest."

Not that he'd be free even then, I thought. At least, not from himself.

6

MARTIN DIDN'T HAVE MUCH to say after my monologue. It was possible that what I'd said had depressed him, or that he didn't believe me—both of which were normal reactions to me opening my mouth. In either case, I might as well have been talking to a wall.

It was about nine in the evening, and I'd had enough of his company. "It's time for me to leave," I told Martin.

"You sure?"

"Yes." I poured the remaining beer down my throat. "See you. Maybe." I got up and went to pay the bill.

After leaving the bar, I walked the rain-slicked streets of Old Town for a while, smoking cigarettes. At the Town Hall Square, I saw how hundreds of colored lights from the nearby restaurants reflected off the wet cobblestones, merging into each other and transforming the square into a kind of abstract painting.

I eventually found myself in front of a bar called Nowhere. Above the bar door hung a red light, illuminating the steps leading down to the entrance. As the rain started getting stronger, I decided to step inside.

The ceiling of the underground bar consisted of

large stone arches. It had probably been used as a storage room for grain a long time ago. For some reason, I had always liked the atmosphere of the place. Perhaps because it reminded me of a catacomb.

When I walked to the old wooden bar counter, I recognized the bartender with curly hair and glasses serving drinks behind it. He had once told me that he was an art student. Considering he was still working there, it seemed that art didn't pay much. Unless of course you drew triangles or smudges and had somehow gotten a millionaire's patronage.

I sat down in front of the counter and ordered a Bloody Mary. The bartender didn't recognize me. Or pretended he didn't. The shelves lined with alcohol bottles behind him were reflective. After he had served me my drink, I looked at the reflection of my face. It wasn't an unattractive one. But neither was it a happy one. In fact, the longer I looked at it, the more I saw the torment writ upon it. Or was I just imagining it? Thoughts painted reality, after all. Of course, at the same time, reality painted thoughts.

But where had it all gone wrong for me? I must have been happy once. Or at least content. What was it that had pushed me over the edge into the land of hopelessness in which I now wandered? I suppose it had been many things. However, it all seemed to have started with school. I *hated* going to school, you see. I even had to repeat the ninth grade. Not to mention that I dropped out of high school.

The school system, as I had experienced it, seemed to have consisted mostly of brainwashing in an attempt to destroy a person's individuality, creativity, and ability to question things. It was not intended to enlighten anyone or to make them into critical thinkers. It didn't teach you how to think; it only taught you what to think. Schools appeared to exist only in order to indoctrinate people to accept the authority and mindless routine that was the rule in our nine-to-five society.

In fact, when I read about the history of the school system, I found that it dated back to the Middle Ages and was originally designed to teach people religion. And what did religious people do? They embraced utterly absurd ideas without any skeptical thinking whatsoever. And the same system that was designed to brainwash them—full of rote learning, non-questioning, obedience to authority, and punishment—was the same system still in use today. Why? Because it worked. At least for the most part. For some reason, it hadn't worked on me.

I therefore had no choice but to educate myself. And that's exactly what I did. I spent numerous years isolating myself from the world, reading philosophy and taking long walks in nature in order to let the words settle. What I soon discovered was that there were many ways how one could look at things, which was the opposite of what they taught you in school. And that the views which prevailed at any given time were not dependent on truth, but on power.

Naturally, philosophy soon led me to science. After all, the latter had developed from the former. And what I discovered was that many of the ideas in philosophy were now hopelessly outdated and long overridden by scientific advances, which of course didn't stop backwards academics from continuing to discuss the utterly obsolete ideas of Aristotle and Plato, as though they still had any relevance.

The more I learned about science, the more it seemed to be the key to understanding everything, and I soon came to believe that there was nothing it couldn't solve. I even went back to high school for a while, though this only lasted for about a year until I dropped out again because the kind of science that I was interested in—a way of looking at *everything*—was not being taught or even appreciated in school. And so, I continued my studies alone.

Eventually, however, I began to see a huge problem with science. Although it promised to explain everything and solve all of the world's problems, even a cursory glance at the world showed that it had far less power than its proponents thought. This was because humans, by nature, weren't science-minded beings. We had evolved in an age of no science, where everything appeared like magic to us. And so, instead of chemistry, we preferred alchemy. Instead of astronomy, we preferred astrology. Instead of atheism, we preferred religion. And instead of the truth, we preferred comforting lies.

Although the whole world was materialistic and without meaning, with science and technology we could theoretically accomplish *anything*. The question was—why hadn't we? Why was the world in practice still such a miserable fucking shithole? Why were we forced to spend such a large part of our lives studying things we couldn't have cared less about and would never remember? Why were we forced to slave our entire lives away at jobs we hated? Why were we expected to take part in endless societal delusions which someone had just made up? Why were we constantly surrounded by so much stupidity and superficiality, corruption and crime, greed and poverty, inequality and hunger, misery and disease, mental illness and suffering, violence and torture, war and senseless death?

Most scientists seemed to be either delusional optimists who had made a religion out of their profession, or just average people for whom it was only a job. Few of them used the scientific method on society and human life. Yet if science was about finding out what was true, wasn't *everything* supposed to be looked at scientifically? Including religion, traditions, and the socioeconomic system. And when one *did* examine these scientifically, it became painfully obvious that there was very little truth in any of them and yet they were the chains by which we had all been imprisoned. And what's worse, most of us *wanted* to be imprisoned by them.

Which is why the core of our society had been the

same since the Sumerians invented agriculture twelve thousand years ago, when the first cities emerged around the first farmlands. Those cities were very similar to today's cities—full of poor people ruled over by a rich elite. The poor did all the monotonous and dirty work, from which the rich profited. And when you were born rich, you could only become richer because the rich had built mechanisms into society which made this possible—the divine right of kings, lending money, investing, buying up real estate, and so on.

If, on the other hand, you had made the mistake of being born poor, society was designed against you in such a way as to keep you poor forever. The only consolations you had whilst poor were religion and traditions—which were just another invention of the rich to keep you under control—as well as having children, the purpose of which was to create new slaves for the rich.

The goal of the rich had always been the same throughout history—to establish their dominion and to enslave everyone else. Perhaps that was a simplified way of looking at things, but it was essentially the truth. It always had been. And it always would be. For humans were by nature fundamentally selfish beings who ultimately did not care about anything but their own well-being.

For obvious reasons, too much critical thinking in society was not good for the rich, because otherwise people might start seeing through their deceptions and begin to rebel—as happened, for instance, during the French Revolution. That's why science that benefited the rich—such as the creation of medicine for so-called mental illness, which brought in billions of dollars each year and kept people under control—was widely practiced. Whereas science that would lift people out of poverty and make them into critical thinkers, was not—for who would the rich then use as their slaves?

It was after learning all these things that I started asking myself whether there was anything that went *beyond* science. Something that could explain the nature of the world without being influenced by delusional optimism or a slave mentality. Something that would question *everything*, including that which was considered taboo, such as the value of human life.

And so, I went back to philosophy. However, my usual philosophers, such as Nietzsche, Rousseau, Voltaire, Montaigne, and even Diogenes, didn't go far enough for me anymore in their skepticism. What I needed were philosophers who were willing to follow the truth to the bitter end. Even if it shattered our most beloved illusions. Even if it brought us on the heights of despair. Even if it made a hell out of our world. And such philosophers, indeed, I eventually found: Hegesias, Al-Ma'arri, Chamfort, Schopenhauer, Leopardi, Bahnsen, Mainländer, Hartmann, Zapffe, Cioran, Horstmann, Gray, Benatar, Ligotti.

Although there weren't many of them, they had always existed somewhere in the shadows of human history. Their philosophy was known as philosophical pessimism. And they had very little good to say about *anything*. Which was why they had never achieved much mainstream fame, given that most people did not want their illusions destroyed since their illusions were the only thing that gave their lives meaning. Whereas these philosophers were all about destroying illusions, including our most cherished ones. They said exactly what I had been suspecting for a while now—that the world was not a good place, that it was not created for us, that life had no purpose or meaning, and that it was full of senseless suffering. In other words—that it would have been better never to have been born.

After realizing that life was not a blessing but a curse, I concluded that there was only one sensible thing left for humanity to do, which was to go voluntarily extinct. And I was far from the first to have suggested it. In fact, there were many like me in the world, though we usually kept our views hidden for obvious reason.

Because the idea that existence was something good, that it was meaningful, and that it should be perpetuated indefinitely was so deeply ingrained into most of us that nearly everybody accepted it without question. For if you seriously considered, even if but for one moment, that it would have been better never to have been, it would cast doubt on *everything* you have ever believed in. And most people had neither the courage nor intellect for such consideration. For them, life was simple. You did what you were told and pretended you were happy about it. Because after you died, you went to heaven, where everything was fine forever.

Of course, the discovery of such grim truths had dire consequences for me—constant depression, despair, and alienation from human society. It was as if I had opened Pandora's box and my world would never be the same again. The naive pleasures of the average person, such as anniversaries, marriage, children, and a career, fell into ashes before me, and every time I had to face them anywhere in the world, I was filled with disgust.

And so, I soon became to despise the world on an almost daily basis, constantly wishing I had never been born. Yet nevertheless, I didn't have the strength to end my life. Either I was a coward, or I still held onto some part of the one thing that didn't manage to escape from Pandora's box—hope.

This I pondered when someone suddenly sat next to me in the bar. It was a woman in black.

7

THE WOMAN IN BLACK seemed quite drunk. She asked me what I was drinking.

"Alcohol," I answered.

She gave a sarcastic smile. "Smartass."

"That's me."

"Then why are you sitting here all alone?"

"Too smart I guess."

"Or maybe not smart enough?"

"Maybe." I finished my drink.

"You want another one?"

"Sure."

"What do you want?"

"How about a Bloody Mary?"

"Okay."

She ordered two Bloody Marys. We sat in silence whilst the bartender mixed up the drinks.

"So what brings you here?" she asked, taking a sip from her cocktail.

"My feet," I said, taking a sip from the Bloody Mary, the smell of Tabasco and black pepper tickling my nostrils.

"Very funny. But really?"

"Got no place to go and going there tomorrow," I

quoted from an old movie. I guess I didn't know how to talk to people.

"Okay okay, mister mysterious." She gestured with her hands. "Are you a magician?"

"I was."

She raised her eyebrows. "Oh? Were you able to make something disappear?"

"Yeah. My will to live."

"Oh, hush now." She put her finger on my lips. "None of that kind of talk. Why don't you offer me a cigarette instead?"

"All right. Do you want a cigarette?"

"I thought you'd never ask."

We took our drinks upstairs to the smoking area and sat down. I opened my pack of Marlboro Red and extended it to her. We both lit up.

"You're weird," she said, letting out a puff of smoke.

"Am I?"

"Yes." She put her hand on my leg and moved it towards my crotch. "But attractive."

After we were finished with our cigarettes, she asked me whether she could push her tongue down my throat.

"All right," I said, after which she attacked me with it like a snake. Her mouth tasted like cigarettes and alcohol. But so did mine. She moved her tongue around my mouth for a while, as if searching for something—perhaps the meaning of life—and then finally pulled it out.

"Wanna go to my place?" she asked.

"Okay."

We got up and walked downstairs. Before leaving the bar, she pushed me into a dark corner, shoved her hand down my pants and wrapped it around my cock, which immediately got hard. She played with it whilst I took out my phone and ordered a taxi. She was too drunk to order it herself.

After the taxi arrived, it took us about ten minutes to arrive at our destination. We entered the nondescript building where she lived, took the elevator to the top floor, and walked to her apartment door. She fumbled with the keys for a bit before she got the door open.

It was a penthouse apartment, not far from the harbor. Looking out the window, I could see the sea in the distance. "Nice place," I commented.

"It's not mine," she said, struggling to remove her knee-high boots. "I'm only borrowing it for a while."

We sat behind the kitchen table. She brought out a bottle of white wine and poured us both a glass. I wasn't a fan of white wine, but I took it. We sipped on the wine in silence.

"So," I finally asked, "are we gonna have sex?"

"What do *you* think?" she said teasingly.

By the time we were done with the wine, she looked as though she was about to lose consciousness at any moment.

"I'm gonna go to the bedroom," she said, stumbling up from her seat. I followed her.

She sat on the bed and sluggishly started taking off her clothes. She removed her shirt but left her bra on. While she was trying to pull her jeans and panties off, however, she suddenly fell asleep. It didn't seem as though she was going to come to before the morning.

Since I was drunk and tired, I decided to lie down next to her. From my vantage point, I could partly see her shaved vagina. It looked inviting. What a shame, I thought.

I observed her body for a while until I drifted off to sleep.

8

I HAD AN ERECTION. Next to me lay a woman who looked like Vicky. After caressing her for a while, I climbed on top of her and removed her panties. But when I attempted to penetrate her, I wasn't able to. I tried again a few more times unsuccessfully before I finally lifted the blanket, only to see that her vagina had been sewn shut.

I opened my eyes. The woman next to me was awake. "You look much younger than you did last night," she said.

In daylight, with her makeup smudged and without the influence of alcohol, I could see that she was much older than she had looked like the night before. In fact, she must have been at least ten years older than me. She was still attractive though.

"Did we have sex last night?" she asked coyly.

"I'm afraid not," I said, trying to hide my disappointment.

She frowned. "Are you sure?"

"Yes. You fell asleep whilst taking off your pants."

"Oh, so that's why my ass was bare . . ."

There was an awkward silence.

"Listen, I'm gonna go take a quick shower," she

eventually said. "I'll be right back." She got up and left the room.

The clock on the wall said it was nine in the morning. I checked my phone; it had a text message from Vicky. "Sorry, I was working," it said. I wasn't surprised; she was a veterinary assistant and often worked long hours, including night shifts. "We can have steak together," the message continued. "How about one in the afternoon at the place we were supposed to go to?"

"All right," I texted back to her. "I'll meet you there."

The woman soon returned to the room, wearing only a towel over her, her large breasts half-visible.

"I guess I should leave, right?" I asked.

"I'm afraid so. My mother's coming over soon."

I started getting up from the bed.

"Wait a minute," she said. "I can't let you leave empty-handed."

I began to get excited, hoping she was referring to a blowjob. Instead, she took a small tin box from a nearby shelf and said, "I'll give you a tarot reading."

Again, I tried to hide my disappointment. "A . . . tarot reading?"

"Yes. I recently bought a new deck but I've yet to try it on anyone. Before using it, you see, you need to recharge it with energy through a special ritual. Otherwise, it can be dangerous. Well, I've done the ritual and I wanna see if it worked."

Although I knew that tarot was bullshit, I saw no

harm in humoring her. "I don't really believe in that kind of stuff but go ahead."

She shuffled the cards and put them on the bed. "I want you to cut the deck three times."

After I cut the deck three times, she took the top card and turned it over. "The Fool. It usually symbolizes new beginnings. But yours is reversed, which is not a good sign."

She took another one. "The Devil. Although it *can* be good, yours is upright, signifying downfall."

She drew the third card. "The Hanged Man. Hmm, strange. I'm not sure the ritual worked."

"Why not?"

"Because it's the third bad card in a row. If it were upright, it would mean improvement. But yours is reversed, indicating bad decisions and being trapped."

"Beginner's misfortune."

She took the fourth card from the deck, looking a little flustered. "I have to redo the ritual. The cards seem to be negatively charged."

I looked at the card and smiled. It was Death. "Seems to be working just fine to me," I said, getting up from the bed. "Can I use your bathroom before I leave?"

"Of course." She started putting the cards away.

I went to the bathroom. It smelled like someone had taken a hangover shit in there; it was foul. I took a piss, washed my face, put some water in my disheveled hair and brushed it back with a hairbrush I found on the counter.

She was standing by the front door when I came out of the bathroom, still wearing only the towel over her. After I put on my shoes and coat, she suddenly put her arms around me and kissed me on the lips. "We'll fuck some other time," she whispered into my ear before I left.

I doubted it.

9

THE AIR FELT COLD when I stepped out of the building. The city was quiet. It was Sunday.

I lit a cigarette. Since I had a few hours to kill before meeting Vicky, I decided to go and sit down somewhere. I started walking towards Dublin. I guess I had no imagination.

When I got to the pub, I ordered a beer at the counter and sat down in the same spot as the day before. As I sipped on my beer, I overheard two people nearby talking about Stalin and Russian society. Everyone's an expert on things they know little about. Somehow, their conversation went from that to relationships and cheating. It seemed to me that the girl was flirting with the guy. The guy told her that he still talked to his ex, even though she had cheated on him. The girl said he shouldn't. The guy eventually invited the girl over to London where he lived. The girl said it was too expensive. An empty pleasantry followed by a lie. As is most of human conversation.

I went to the bathroom. Whilst pissing into the urinal, I noticed that someone had written the word "hubris" on the wall in front of me. A strange thing to write on a bathroom wall, I thought. But apt. Because, after all, wasn't that the whole problem? The hubris of humanity. Everybody was so damn sure of what they were and what surrounded them. There was so little doubt in them. Everybody was so self-important and self-obsessed, yet few were self-aware. The belief that their lives were meaningful and good rarely went into question. Most people thought that they were powerful individuals who were capable of accomplishing anything they set their minds to. When in truth they accomplished nothing. They died stupid as they lived. With nothing to show for it in the end. It was only their overconfidence that made their lives bearable. And this was their hubris. Without it, would there ever have been a society?

As I was washing my hands, I recalled something that Bukowski had said: "Realize how ridiculous we are with our intestines wound round, shit slowly running through as we look each other in the eyes and say, 'I love you.' We're monstrosities." As usual when it came to his observations on humanity, he was spot on. We *were* monstrosities. And we were full of shit. Both figuratively and literally.

I went back to my table and sat down. The girl and guy who had sat nearby were gone. I looked out the window. The yellow leaves were beginning to fall. For lack of anything better to do, I took out *Will O' the Wisp*.

I took a sip of beer and started reading:

"But you don't look as much in pain as you were a few days ago. Do you still have any pains?"

"I do not have pains. I am in permanent pain."

I read a couple of chapters before my mind started drifting and I began thinking about the lady I had left in the apartment. Not that she could have helped me. Not that anyone could. It seemed that all she was looking for was a quick fuck and even that didn't work out. And though I wouldn't have said no to that, what I needed more was somebody to take care of me. To look after me. For I couldn't always rely on doing that myself. I was self-destructive. And I needed somebody to counterbalance that. But the person that was supposed to do that was gone.

Well, that wasn't quite right. She wasn't *supposed* to do anything. It had just seemed to me that she had understood why I was the way I was, that she had accepted it, and that I didn't need to pretend around her. At least that was the impression she had given in the beginning. Yet in the end it was all too much for her. Whatever charm I'd had had worn off over time and she had stopped loving me.

She had stayed together with me for such a long time only because she had nothing better to do with her time. But then she had found a job as a veterinary assistant, and suddenly she didn't need me at all anymore because she had found something else to fill the void in her heart. Something better. And I became redundant. Which was something I couldn't really blame her for since I wasn't always easy to live with. My behavior was often unpredictable, especially when drunk, which I frequently was. I was extremely negative and critical about everything around me. Not to mention constantly depressed.

And now that she was no longer there, the darkness inside of me was kept at bay by no one. I felt that it was going to consume me.

10

IT WAS ALMOST TIME to meet Vicky, so I left the pub and bought some cigarettes from a nearby kiosk.

I walked the streets of Old Town towards the steakhouse where we were supposed to meet. We had planned to go there right before breaking up and then never did. It was strange how people did so many things together and then from a certain point onwards didn't anymore. It all seemed rehearsed somehow and fake. Perhaps it was because we had invented relationships. We had made them up. They weren't real things like the sun and moon were real. They were ideas with fictional rules. And that's why they didn't work. The real world always got in the way.

When I arrived at the restaurant, I leaned against the terrace and lit a cigarette. The name of the restaurant was Liha ja Vein—for me, Viha ja Lein.[*]

It was a little chilly to wait outside, but I didn't mind. I had always liked autumn. Standing there, smoking my cigarette, I suddenly recalled an idea I had once had for a novel which was to take place during autumn. It was going to be about a suicidal young

---

[*] This wordplay only works in Estonian: Liha ja Vein = Meat and Wine; Viha ja Lein = Hate and Grief.

painter and her attempts to find a reason to survive in a world that didn't give a shit.

To be sure, it was a lousy idea. Just like all the other ideas I'd had for novels, none of which ever materialized. I never did much with this one either except for writing a few bad chapters and deciding that the main character's name should be Lola, a decision which took me hours to arrive at. However, I still liked the title I had come up for it, which was *The Occluded Front*, a meteorological term which is used when a cold front overtakes a warm front. The title was supposed to reflect the protagonist's mental state. At the moment, it appeared to reflect mine.

Eventually Vicky showed up, fifteen minutes late. I noticed that she had dyed her hair blonde.

"Hi," she said.

"Hello."

"Sorry for being late."

"That's all right." It was strange for me to see her. I wondered whether it was also strange for her to see me. "Shall we go inside?"

We sat by the window and took off our coats. Vicky was wearing a white T-shirt which had a picture of a praying mantis on it along with the phrase, "I'm praying for you." Pretty clever, I thought.

I looked around. The interior of the restaurant seemed rather tasteless and gaudy on account of the LCD "fireplace," faux marble, and bright red carpets. I assumed that it was owned by Russians.

A waitress came over. She had a Russian accent. We ordered some beer and strip steaks.

"So . . . how's it going?" Vicky asked me soon after the waitress had left. I sensed as though she thought she had to and not that she really wanted to.

"Not so good," I said with an anguished smile. "Not so good at all."

"I'm sorry."

Are you?

The waitress brought us our beers.

I took a sip of beer. "What about you? How's your life been going?"

"I'm actually doing great." She gave a wry smile. "Sorry, I know that's not what you wanted to hear."

"Nah, that's good."

For you. Not for me.

We sat in silence for a while until the waitress brought us our steaks.

"How's it going with your job?" I asked, chewing on a piece of meat.

"It's going good. How's yours?"

"It sucks, as usual. You were lucky to be able to find a job that interests you. Not an easy thing to do in this world."

"Tell me about it."

"Anything else interesting happen in your life lately?"

"Actually, yes. I just got back from Spain a few days ago."

I feigned interest. "And how was it?"

"It was really nice. We stayed at this small town in the mountains and went hiking every day."

"Sounds nice. Who did you go with?"

"Just a colleague from work." It looked like she wanted to change the topic. "How about you? Anything interesting happen in your life?"

I thought for a moment. "Well, one night I got really drunk whilst playing five finger fillet and I managed to stab one of my fingers with the knife. Of course, this wasn't the first time that has happened." I held up my hand to show her the scars. "However, on this particular occasion I must have hit a vein since it began bleeding quite heavily and every time I bent my finger blood came squirting out of it. Which was kinda hilarious if you think about it."

She didn't say anything after that. But her expression said it all. You need help, it said. Serious help. Unfortunately, I didn't believe in psychiatry. As far as I was concerned, all so-called mental illness—with the possible exception of schizophrenia—was a completely natural reaction to our environment. Because after all, what could be more natural than being depressed in a world like this? But of course, that wasn't the mainstream view. And I'd had numerous arguments with Vicky regarding this in the past.

I was about halfway done with my steak before I could take it no longer. "This steak has way too much fat," I said. "In fact, nearly half of it is fucking fat.

What the fuck? What am I paying thirty euros for? Why is everything in this world only half of what is advertised? Or less."

"Yeah, it's not the best I've had either," she said nonchalantly.

Of course, the problem wasn't so much the steak; the problem was Vicky. Meeting her had been a mistake. She had clearly moved on with her life, whereas I hadn't. And I felt even more depressed after meeting her than I had before. Story of my life.

"Well, this steak was about as fucked as was meeting you," I said after we were finished. "Let me ask you something, why did you decide to meet me?"

"Because I wanted to eat steak."

"You could have done that alone."

"I thought you wanted to see me."

"But did you want to see me?"

She remained silent. I already knew the answer. I dug some cash out of my wallet, threw it on the table, and got up. "I'm leaving. So long."

Outside, I lit a cigarette and walked away. Unsurprisingly, she did not follow me. Perhaps I had been rude, but I simply couldn't talk to her. It felt suffocating. It was clear that I meant nothing to her anymore. That the three years we had spent together meant nothing at all to her anymore. And that I was still a prisoner of the past.

Alone and with a big fucking hole in my heart, I walked onwards to the next bar, deciding to get as drunk as humanly possible. Because when you were drunk, you felt less pain about the world. Although you might get nauseous, it was better than being conscious.

11

I WAS ON MY way towards a bar on the outskirts of Old Town called Scarlet Emperor when I suddenly stopped walking.

On the pavement before me stood a raven on top of a bloodied pigeon, pecking at its lifeless carcass. The pigeon's feathers were ruffled, its heart and other organs were missing, and bits of bone were sticking out. Only the head and wings were still there.

The raven lifted its head and looked towards me for a moment before it continued pecking.

I walked on.

12

DESPITE ITS NAME, SCARLET Emperor was a rather trashy-looking place, resembling more a skatepark than an actual bar. And yet it held a certain rugged charm to it. It was unpretentious. Besides, I had been there plenty of times in the past and had met some interesting people.

Since the bar was next to a hostel where lots of backpackers and travelers stayed, it was often visited by "exotic" patrons. And I usually preferred to converse with them more than with my fellow countrymen, who rarely seemed to have anything interesting to say.

A few of the people who frequented the place even knew me there. One Turkish guy always used to call me professor, probably because of my tendency to descend into long monologues about various things that I found interesting or idiotic, mostly the latter. Unfortunately, when I entered the bar this time around, I didn't see any familiar faces.

I bought a beer from the goth bartender with cheek piercings and went into the smoking room. It was empty. I lit a cigarette. For lack of anything better to do, I began examining the graffiti on the walls.

CAPITALISM = SHIT. Okay, I thought, but what do

you replace it with? FUCK THE SYSTEM! Sure, but then what? LOVE IS AN ILLUSION. Yeah, a neurochemical one, just like happiness. GO CRAZY AAH! Already on my way there, buddy. IF ONLY I'D GET FUCKED AS MUCH AS I GET BEATEN UP. Well, I don't know about you, but life already fucks me plenty. THE FIRST STEP TO ETERNAL LIFE IS THAT YOU HAVE TO DIE. Only if you become famous after death, which isn't very useful. STOP DRINKING ALCOHOL OR YOU WILL DIE. But what if I want to?

A few people had entered the smoking room whilst I was examining the graffiti. Two of them started talking to each other and a younger woman with short brown hair came to stand near the window with me. She lit a cigarette.

"Have you ever been depressed?" I asked her as I lit another cigarette.

"What?" She looked towards me, apparently caught off guard. "Why would you ask me something like that?"

"Well, why not?"

"Because it's personal."

"Is it? And yet half the world seems to be depressed."

"Yes, but they don't talk about it."

"Maybe that's the problem?"

After blowing out a cloud of smoke, she said, "So you just walk up to random women and talk to them about depression?"

I took a sip of beer. "Not usually, no."

"So what's different today?"

"What's different today is that I don't give a shit."

"Hmm. Sounds like you're depressed." She smiled sardonically. "Perhaps you should seek help?"

"Perhaps indeed." I sucked on my cigarette and blew out a thick puff of smoke. "However, I don't think that being depressed is any less natural than not being depressed. And the same goes for all mental illness."

"What on earth do you mean by that?"

"What I mean is that there is no pathological process in the brain that can cause mental illness. Mental illness is merely a reaction to our environment that is based upon our life experience and knowledge. So when a person gets depressed, for instance, it is his life experience and knowledge telling him that things aren't actually as good as he has been led to believe in our society of head-in-the-sand optimism. And it is this discrepancy between expectation and reality that causes depression."

"Oh really? Then what about the people who get depressed without a reason?"

I let out a puff of smoke and chuckled. "You mean happy people that get depressed?"

"Yes."

"There's no such people."

She wrinkled her nose. "Bullshit."

"Oh, I'm sure you think they're happy. Perhaps

they also think they're happy. But most of the brain works unconsciously. So even if they've lied enough to that small conscious part of themselves to believe that everything is fine and everything is dandy, it is in fact the unconscious part of the brain telling itself that it is not actually fine, and their seemingly causeless depression is a sign of that."

"That doesn't sound very plausible."

"Okay. Then how about this. Depression is simply an evolutionary mishap because millions of years ago humans evolved in a world where they were too preoccupied with survival, instead of getting to know the world. And now that we're not so busy surviving anymore and possess so much more knowledge than our brains were meant for, we are slowly beginning to realize that our survival actually has no point because we exist in a world that has neither any purpose nor meaning. And *that's* where depression comes from. From *this* realization and not some 'chemical imbalance.' "

There was silence. I lit up another cigarette. "Do you want one?"

"No thanks," she said. "I think I'm done with you." She turned around and left the room.

Oh well. It wasn't as though I wasn't used to her reaction by now. I had been telling people the same thing for many years and their reaction had almost always been the same. Pessimistic thinking just wasn't fashionable; only its opposite was. This was why, as Ligotti put it, there were at any given time more cannibals than philosophical pessimists. And (un)fortunately I had almost nothing positive to say. About anything.

A few new people entered the smoking room, but they didn't seem interested in me. After I had finished the cigarette and beer, I exited the room and went back to the bar counter. I sat down on a bar stool and ordered another beer and a shot of whiskey. I downed the whiskey and started drinking the beer.

Not far from me sat a bearded guy and a young girl who I assumed was his girlfriend. I asked them whether they minded my company. They said they didn't. So I decided to chit-chat with them a bit, holding back the things I really wanted to talk about, such as the futility of all human life for instance.

"So what brings you here?" I asked.

"Oh we're just visiting some of our favorite bars in Tallinn," the guy said. "We're from Tartu."

"Ah, Tartu . . ." I tried to recall something about Tartu from when I still used to frequent it on account of an ex-girlfriend. "You ever been to a rock bar there called Subterranean?"

"Of course. Great place! Excellent selection of music."

"Yeah, and those one-liter beers, man . . . I used to visit it all the time back in the day."

"And you don't anymore?"

"Well, it was the favorite bar of an ex-girlfriend and I'm afraid I'll run into her there."

"Understandable. That reminds me, we were actually planning on going to that rock bar on Tatari street after this round. What was the name of the place?" He looked towards the girl who had so far been silent.

"Stock . . . something," she said.

"Stockwood?" I offered.

"That's the one." I had been there many times. Aside from the occasional customer who threatened to beat you up it was an all-right place. Unpretentious. As rock bars tended to be.

"In that case, do you mind if I tag along?" I asked.

"Not at all," the guy said. "The more the merrier!"

I couldn't tell whether he was just being polite or if he indeed didn't mind. But I was desperate for some company. Any kind of company.

After finishing our drinks, we left the bar. It was dark and cold outside and slightly rainy. I lit a cigarette and followed the couple. The city was empty. As it tended to be on Sunday evenings. For some reason, society had deemed it acceptable to get shit-faced on Fridays and Saturdays, but not on other days. I guess it was to keep us in line.

Aside from the rock bar, Tatari street held an all-night pizza joint, a hookah bar, a sex shop-cum-adult theater, a gay dance club, and a sex club. I had visited four out of the five.

When we stepped into the bar, Black Sabbath's "Killing Yourself to Live" was playing in the background. Good choice, I thought. The bar had a red and black décor and the lights that hung overhead were made out of real drums. On the walls were written the names of various Estonian rock bands along with the years in which they were formed. I didn't recognize most of them. No one did.

We ordered some beers from the bar and sat down at a booth with red vinyl seats. My companions began talking about some music festival they were going to go to, which didn't interest me in the slightest. Instead, I focused on my beer and the lyrics of Black Sabbath's "Paranoid" which was now playing in the background. I had always found the lyrics of a song its most important part. And this one's were pertinent.

Soon, a friend of theirs joined our table. Her hair was dyed red, and she looked like she was barely twenty. The three of them started talking with each other and I was beginning to feel left out, as always. For some reason, people rarely seemed to show any interest in me. It was usually me that had to intrude upon them. Perhaps it was my lack of confidence. Or my apathetic face. In either case, it seemed as though people could somehow sense that I wasn't like them.

A guy that looked like a typical Estonian, who'd been drinking alone in the bar so far, suddenly came to our table and asked if he could join us. "The more the merrier," the bearded guy said again, and the person immediately joined their conversation. How had it been so easy for him, I wondered?

I emptied my beer and went to order another one.

"Who wants to go for a cigarette?" the girl with red

hair asked when I got back.

"I wouldn't mind one," I said.

It looked like the others were busy with their conversation, so the two of us went outside. We lit our cigarettes near the entrance of the bar.

"So what brings you out?" she asked. Everybody always asked the same questions.

"An impending sense of doom," I replied.

"Aww. Are you feeling depressed?"

"Indeed I am."

"Do you want a hug?"

"Why not."

She hugged me for five seconds.

"Thanks," I said after her body had separated from mine.

Ultimately, however, it seemed to have been an empty gesture. For when we got back to our table, she stopped paying attention to me, and I continued sipping on my beer alone. Well, that's how it was in this world. Depressed, negative, and pessimistic people were often treated like lepers. It was as though people feared catching what they had. Perhaps because what they were saying made sense? Hell, if everybody would see the world as it truly was, we'd all be depressed. But if that were the case, then there wouldn't even be any people. For no one would dare yank another soul out of non-existence and imprison them inside this miserable prison of flesh in order to suffer and die. The fact that we kept on breeding showed that delusion was necessary for the continuation of the species, even as there was no necessity to continue the species.

In the meantime, a few more random people had joined our table, and it was getting harder and harder for me to endure their inane and empty chatter, which, as always, was mostly about themselves. Eventually I couldn't hold back any longer, so I started telling the guy next to me—the one that looked like a typical Estonian—how things weren't nearly as good as we had been led to believe. How the truth was that most of us would never become successful or find a soulmate or even be happy for any meaningful length of time because such ideas came from fiction, from Hollywood movies with happy endings. The real world didn't work that way. In the real world, most people worked their fingers to the bone and had nothing to show for it in the end. They had a series of miserable relationships with people they had nothing in common with, which ended in heartache and despair, sometimes even in murder. And they never achieved the happiness they so desperately sought because happiness was like a mirage in the desert—it evaporated before you could ever reach it.

"In conclusion," I said, "everything we do is ultimately futile and based on delusions."

"Hmm," the guy next to me murmured before finishing his beer in one gulp. "I applaud your courage in saying all that, but it all sounds a bit too bleak for me. I like to think that life is more what you make of it."

After that, he turned his attention towards one of the young girls, clearly not interested anymore in hearing me bitch about the shortcomings of reality. Because hey, who needs pessimism when you've got pussy.

Alone and ignored again, I observed the others around me. The bearded guy seemed particularly happy for some reason since he soon ordered champagne for everybody. It appeared as though he was celebrating simply being alive, which was something I tended to mourn. Hell, that was the reason I drank so much. It seemed we both drank for the same thing but for opposite reasons.

When the bartender came to our table with the glasses of champagne, everybody took one but me. The bearded guy then stood up, lifted his glass into the air and said, "To good drink and good company!"

I wondered whether his toast included me.

The rest of the table then got up as well and started raising their glasses. But when they brought the glasses together, they did it with such drunken vigor that all of the glasses shattered on impact as champagne and shards of glass came raining down on the table.

It was like some drunken Last Supper, I thought, observing the chaos before me.

And I felt like Judas.

13

IT WAS AROUND THREE in the morning, and I was on my way home in a taxi. I had ordered it right after the champagne fiasco. Nobody had even noticed me leave.

The taxi driver was staring at me in the rearview mirror. "Do you like heavy metal by any chance?" he asked.

"That's the only kind I like," I replied.

He put on some generic rock music on the car stereo. "You know, I used to be the drummer in a black metal band called Delusion back in the day."

"Is that so? Did the band's name indicate the likelihood of making it as a black metal band in today's world?"

He didn't say anything in response.

After I got out of the taxi, I smoked a cigarette in front of the stairwell to my apartment, looked into the mailbox, which was empty, and finally dragged myself up the stairs. I didn't like living there anymore. Not after Vicky left. But finding a new apartment and moving was an ordeal I had neither the interest nor energy for. Besides, it hardly mattered in the end where you rotted away. All homes were ultimately graves.

I entered my apartment, took off my shoes and

coat, put on some music, and plopped down on the couch. The song which began aggressively blasting from the speakers was called "I Still Drink Alone" by a Norwegian rock band called The Cumshots. It was one of my favorites.

We all have our demons,
Mine is sobriety
These four walls, that's my society

I was done with people for the day. As always, they made me feel even worse. However, I wasn't nearly done with drinking yet. Alcohol was my oldest friend after all. And even though it was the kind of friend that was a bad influence, that never made me want to improve myself, it nevertheless allowed me to *remain* myself, which was not something I could say about any group of people I had ever had the displeasure of meeting.

A toothless dog don't need a bone
I'm sorry, mom
I still drink alone

I got up from the couch and located a half-liter bottle of Jim Beam, which I had hidden on the bookshelf. It was an old trick of alcoholics to hide a few bottles around the house so that there would always be a spare in case you happened to run out at the wrong time—

for instance, when you were still conscious.

I took the bottle to the couch, uncorked it, and took a hit. It felt good. It was one of the few things that did. The bottle had stood next to my collection of Dan Fante books. Like most good authors, Dan had been an alcoholic and the books he wrote were based on his own fucked up life. Eventually, however, Dan was able to stop drinking because he had found God, the likelihood of which happening in my case was close to zero.

In fact, if I had to choose some mythical being as the creator of the world, then it could only be the Devil, which a quick glance at human history clearly implied. A religious sect in the Middle Ages called the Cathars had even believed that the physical world was indeed created by the Devil, for no merciful God could have possibly created something so sick and so vile—it was, after all, the age of the plague. Which was not to say that the world was any less sick now; it was merely sick in different ways. The followers of Catharism were usually burned at the stake by the Inquisition, which, ironically, proved their point. For hell, as Shakespeare wrote, was empty and all the devils were here.

I took a hit of whiskey.

Sitting there and brooding, my eyes came to a stop upon an empty spot in the living room where Vicky's cat tree had stood. Although I hadn't liked her cat, Vicky had been the only person I had been able to communicate with without holding back. At least at the beginning. For her personality had changed over time. Although she had started out as fucked up as me, it turned out that deep inside she had still wanted to live a normal life, so she eventually "grew out of it". Whereas I never did. And my negativity, bitterness, and self-destructiveness eventually became too much for her to handle. And after she left, I did what I always did in such cases—I became even more negative, bitter, and self-destructive. Although I'd already been drinking regularly, after she left I started drinking every day.

I took a hit of whiskey.

One night, whilst out drinking, I had even found a drinking buddy; a barfly called Joe. Me and him were similar in some ways. He had been recently dumped; I had been recently dumped. He was an alcoholic and I was on my way to becoming one. He was nihilistic and I felt that I was the definition of the word. And I had to admit, we did have some good times together . . . as little as I could remember them through the alcoholic haze. But in the end, as always, I got tired of even him, for he was just a little too unhinged and full of himself for my taste, not to mention constantly broke. It seemed that a misanthrope like me just wasn't meant to have friends. And so, I soon found myself alone again. Or, well, almost alone since I still had my bottle.

I took a long hit of whiskey, accidentally spilling some on my shirt.

But the bottle alone wasn't enough, you see. Worse, it often intensified the fury I felt against mankind and the world. Besides, drinking yourself slowly to death was a sad thing. I could scarcely imagine going on for very long with it. Perhaps it would be better to just end everything in one fell swoop, instead of drawing it out. It would only hurt for a moment and then all of my problems would disappear forever. Whereas with alcohol, it would still hurt constantly. Although it reduced my ability to feel suffering, it didn't do so for very long, and in the end didn't solve any of my problems; in fact, it only added to them. Besides, it was ultimately just postponing the inevitable. The inevitable here being death.

Alcoholics, after all, were usually suicidal people who didn't have the courage to kill themselves. And so they hoped that the alcohol would do the job for them. But the alcohol, more often than not, took a long goddamn time before it completely killed you. And so, you slowly withered away until you were but a husk of your former self.

My eyes were beginning to fall shut. I poured the last of the whiskey down my throat.

"Ah Vicky." I sighed. "Damn you for choosing . . . your goddamn kitty-cat . . . instead of ME!"

I hurled the whiskey bottle towards where the cat tree had stood. It shattered into pieces.

14

I SAW A GIANT praying mantis pounding on drums in the darkness. Suddenly, an even bigger praying mantis appeared from behind the first one and bit off its head. Despite the insect no longer having a head, it continued pounding on the drums.

I opened my eyes. Someone was aggressively pounding his fist on my apartment door. I waited for a moment, but the pounding didn't stop.

I wiped the drool from the corner of my mouth and languidly pushed myself up from the couch. The headache I had from the hangover felt like someone was pressing a stiletto heel into my brain.

I maneuvered myself towards the front door, trying to avoid stepping on the shards of glass.

"WHAT DO YOU WANT?"

The answer came back in Russian.

"In Estonian or English."

I got a reply back in broken Estonian. The man behind the door informed me that he had woken up from the noise in my apartment last night. He said it sounded as if someone had thrown in a window.

"I had a small accident, that's all."

He didn't appear to believe me, and I couldn't really

blame him. However, I *was* pissed off that he had woken me up over such a trivial thing. As if I hadn't heard enough noise coming from their apartments over the years—drunken parties, spouses quarreling, drug addicts screaming. It was a Russian neighborhood, after all. And yet he seemed to imply—possibly because I wasn't a Russian—that all the noise was coming from my apartment alone.

He finally mentioned the music.

"Yeah, yeah, I won't listen to it so loudly in the future," I lied. "Now leave me alone."

I turned away from the door and walked into the bathroom to take a piss. I looked in the mirror; I didn't like the person staring back.

Then the phone started ringing. "Oh for fuck's sake! Let me guess. Another telemarketer." Those were the only people who called me anymore.

I went and picked up the phone. "Good morning!" an unnaturally enthusiastic female voice blared in my ear. "I'm calling you from the coin club—" As soon as I heard that I immediately hung up and blocked the number.

My god, I thought. Why was everyone always trying to sell you something? If not things, then ideals and beliefs, religion and hobbies. Or they tried to sell you on how pretty and amazing and successful they were and what a great life they led—or at least pretended to on social media. Whereas, if it was truly so good, why did they need to spend so much time in advertising it?

You did that only if the product you were selling was actually shit. Including if the product was you.

I was getting close to my boiling point. I hadn't gotten nearly enough sleep thanks to the imbecile that had awoken me, and my head was killing me. Worst of all, it was Monday. And though I hated working in general, I particularly hated Mondays when the whole goddamn cycle of slavery began all over again.

I was in desperate need of a cold beer. I walked to the refrigerator and opened it, but it was empty. As I was stepping away from it, I accidentally stepped right onto a sharp piece of glass. "AAAAAAAAAAH! FUCK! FUCKING FUCK!"

I jumped on one leg to the couch and sat down. The shard of glass was still inside my foot. With gritted teeth I pulled it out and removed the sock. Blood flowed from the wound. There were neither any bandages nor gauze in my apartment. There weren't even any paper towels. So I took a wad of toilet paper from the bathroom and pressed it against the wound. I then found some adhesive tape in the desk drawer and pulled it around the toilet paper and my bleeding leg. It'd have to do.

I looked at the time. I was already late for work, and the thought of going to the office and talking with clients about our stupid fucking product filled me with absolute dread. I decided then and there that I'd go to a bar instead. Anybody could be a non-drunk, as Bukowski said, but it took a special talent to be a drunk.

I sent a text message to my boss, claiming that I was ill—which was something I rarely did since I wasn't in the habit of lying. After that, I ate a couple of painkillers for breakfast, brushed my teeth, and got ready to leave.

Each time I stepped out of my apartment, it felt like I was stepping into a mental asylum. Not that it was much better inside, of course; it was just a different kind of madness there.

After I took a seat on the bus, I took out *Will O' the Wisp* and started reading:

> "How is it going?"
> "Terrible."
> "Will you stick it out?"
> "What for? What the hell's to be done with life?"

15

AFTER GETTING OFF THE bus in the city center, I bought a hot dog and a pack of cigarettes from a nearby kiosk.

As I walked towards Old Town, eating my nutritionless hot dog, I considered what kind of bar does one go to on a Monday morning? I wanted a place with few people, something cozy and small, somewhere where they didn't judge you. And there was indeed a place like that in Old Town. Since the bar had no name, people just called it The Place. It had been my favorite bar once, though nowadays I tended to avoid it since it had gotten a bit too crowded. However, there was unlikely to be anyone there on a Monday morning.

After finishing my hot dog, I lit a cigarette. The Gothic spires and towers of Old Town soon came into view in the distance. I had always liked Old Town due to its medieval architecture and winding little cobblestone streets. What I didn't like about it were the endless overpriced restaurants on every corner and a thousand and one pointless little souvenir shops nestled in between. Old Town had over time become a tourist trap and was often an introvert's worst nightmare on account of its constant crowds, especially on the weekend. Fortunately, there were very few people there on a Monday morning.

I soon arrived at The Place. Its entrance was hidden inside an old archway. Like so many buildings in Old Town, it had a vaulted medieval ceiling, and it was furnished by furniture that looked like it was from the 19th century. On one end of the bar stood a big old-fashioned fireplace with large carved columns on either side that looked like lion's feet, which would not have felt out of place inside a castle.

To my surprise, there was already someone in the bar. A gray-haired old man was sitting in an armchair by the fireplace, reading a newspaper, a half-empty glass of beer on a table in front of him. He also had a small dog with him—a Jack Russell if I wasn't mistaken—that was walking around the bar. I crouched down to pet the dog. "Cute dog," I commented. I didn't care for humans much, but dogs I liked.

I walked to the counter and sat on a bar stool. "Hello," I said to the barmaid, who was an older woman.

"Good morning," she said. "What can I get you?"

"Well, a good strong beer wouldn't hurt."

"A good strong beer, huh? How about that one?" She pointed towards a picture on the wall advertising a beer with an alcohol content of eight point six percent.

"That'll do." She took a glass and started pouring the beer from the tap. There was a small aquarium near the bar counter; unlike the last time I had been there, I noticed that there was no fish in it. "What happened to the fish?" I asked.

"Oh the fish? It died." She handed me my beer.

"I'm sorry to hear that." I handed her my debit card.

"Yes, well, everything dies eventually."

"Including hopes and dreams?"

"Even those."

"A shame. Thank you for the beer."

Our transaction complete, the barmaid went to the fireplace near the old man and started building a fire. I wondered whether the old man was her husband.

I took a sip of beer and looked around. The ceiling arch near me was covered with banknotes from various different countries—a common practice in bars which showed that the only true citizen of the world was a drunkard.

Examining the banknotes, I recognized the figures on a number of them: mass-murdering Mao; Queen Elizabeth, the parasite; President Lincoln, the melancholic; President Washington, the slave owner; Khomeini, the inventor of suicide bombing; Churchill, who admired Hitler and Mussolini; Ghandi, the enema aficionado; the severely overrated Nelson Mandela; and Nikola Tesla, who died broke and alone.

Unlike the fairy tales we were told in school, there never were any "great men" in history. They had just been romanticized over time, their achievements grossly exaggerated, with those who helped them or whom they stole from conveniently forgotten, much like their darker side, which rarely was mentioned. But then people always had been in the habit of creating myths, whether they happened to coincide with reality or not. Even though, in truth, even Mother Teresa, who over time has become synonymous with the word saint, was in reality but a fucking fraud. Out of the crooked timber of humanity, as Kant said, no straight thing was ever made.

The wood was crackling in the fireplace and the room was getting warm. I took out *Will O' the Wisp* and started reading:

Are there not always men who turn their backs on life? Is it weakness or strength? Perhaps there was a lot of life in this refusal of life of Alain's. It was for him a way of denying and condemning not life itself, but the aspects of it he hated. Why should he not have yielded to the pangs of his fastidiousness and broken, with no thought of the consequences, with all that displeased him, all that he despised?

16

I WAS ON MY third beer when I put the book away. Having read it before, I knew it had no happy ending. That was one of my favorite things about it. Alain did not magically overcome his difficulties like in some sappy Hollywood movie. The real world didn't work that way. People did not always overcome their difficulties. Often, they succumbed to them. Sometimes they lost their minds and turned to God. Sometimes they became addicted to drugs. And sometimes they committed suicide.

Yet few wrote books or made films like that since that didn't appeal to people. Most people wanted to be lied to. Everything will be all right in the end, they wanted to be told, no matter how bad things currently seem. One day, they would find their soul mate and create the perfect American family. They would find the job of their dreams and become successful beyond belief. They would buy themselves a big house and an expensive car and be happy for the rest of their lives.

Even though in reality it was a hundred times more likely that they would have an unloving relationship with someone they had nothing in common with. That they would create a dysfunctional family—in other words, the average American family—where their children would become estranged from them. That they would waste their lives sitting in an office where they were engaged in monotonous and meaningless tasks that no one even noticed. That they would never differ from the gray masses in any noticeable way. That they would live in a small and dilapidated apartment and use public transport or drive a 1993 Volkswagen Golf (the most popular car in Estonia). And that the only happiness they would ever be able to attain in their pitiful lives was through delirium.

Another book that didn't lie about these things was *Leaving Las Vegas*, which was also close to my heart. Like *Will O' the Wisp*, it featured a doomed protagonist inspired from real life for whom there was no happy ending to his story. Its author John O'Brien had been an alcoholic since his early twenties. And it was said that his alcoholism was the reason why he ended up blowing out his brains. But what was the reason for his alcoholism?

Most people thought that alcoholics were alcoholics because they were addicted to alcohol and that's that. But they were wrong. Addictions arose from trying to fill a hole in your heart; a hole which occurred from having needs that were not met, and perhaps could never be met. And so you filled the hole with temporary palliatives like drugs and alcohol. Unfortunately, you had to keep on filling it and the thing worked less and less over time.

That's where an addiction came from; it had nothing to do with addictive chemicals. No one who lived a happy life—if such people truly existed—decided to suddenly become an alcoholic or a heroin addict. No one. They were always broken people. People who had been broken by a world they never asked to be born into. And since they couldn't live in this world yet couldn't die either, becoming an alcoholic or a drug addict was much like existing between the two, between life and death, which, over time, inevitably shifted towards the latter.

John O'Brien must thus have been suicidal from an early age and his novel reflected his inner torment. In the novel, the protagonist goes to Vegas to drink himself to death. And he succeeds. There's no happy ending, no self-improvement, no overcoming, nothing. Just the blissful peace of non-existence, wherein all of life's problems are finally solved. Which was what the author wanted and got in the end.

I finished my beer and went to the toilet to take a piss. When I came back, I petted the dog, who was by now laying in an armchair.

I ordered another beer. I watched the flames dancing in the fireplace as the barmaid poured it. It was strange how the same thing could be used for both heat and security, as well as for burning people alive. And the same was true of alcohol, which was used for socializing and celebrating, as well as for self-destruction.

I placed the beer on my table, observing as the

bubbles of gas rose to the surface of the glass in an entropic process. If I remembered correctly, I had started drinking alcohol around the age of thirteen, which was quite common in Estonia. Although I wasn't a big drinker at first, the incessant disappointments of life in the course of many fruitless years had ultimately vanquished me and I had often found the bottle as my only companion.

When my first girlfriend, whom I had been together with for four years, left me, I drank a bottle of wine every day for half a year straight. I was only eighteen at the time. Although the amounts weren't nearly as big as I was capable of now, it was drinking with a fixed purpose—to numb the pain. And believe it or not, it worked. Alcohol worked. But only as an alleviative, never as a solution. It was like a painkiller that took away the pain, but only for a while. That's why you had to keep on taking it. Unless of course you fixed that what was causing you pain. But what if it could never be fixed? What if it was like reality, always there? How did you escape from that which never went away? Temporarily, by drugs. Permanently, by death.

Of course, alcohol, like any other drug, had its negative side effects. As I got older, my alcohol consumption grew in proportion to my alcohol tolerance and frustration with life. As grew my extreme behavior whilst drunk. Once upon a time when I had drunk too much in Tartu, for instance, I ended up crawling in a public park and shouting at passersby that I wanted to die. It seemed my disposition hadn't changed much over time.

Nevertheless, I kept on drinking. Was I addicted to the chemicals in the alcohol? No. Was I trying to fill a hole in my heart which over time had only gotten bigger and bigger as life kept chipping more and more pieces off it? Perhaps. And did alcohol help? Sometimes. But was there any drug that cured a disease with a hundred percent efficiency? I could think of only one. And it was reserved for people on death row.

I went over to the fireplace, where smoking was allowed, and lit a cigarette. The dog was sleeping now. I blew out a puff of smoke.

So what was so different about John O'Brien and me? After all, he must have felt at least as hopeless as I did, if not more, yet he had nevertheless managed to create a work of art which brought comfort to those equally disturbed as him—such as me for instance. Yet though I had gotten the alcoholism and suicidal part down, I somehow just couldn't get the writing part down. What was it I lacked? Practice? Inspiration? Passion? Although I had written hundreds of poems and dozens of short stories, finishing an entire novel seemed to me about as simple a task as building the pyramids.

Besides, what did I have to write about? About drinking? About philosophy? About how much I hated the world? Who the hell would want to read about that?

17

I WAS STILL SITTING in the bar when suddenly I got an idea. What if I paid a spontaneous visit to my father? He lived in Helsinki and, if nothing else, the ferry ride there would at least be a change of pace from the monotony of bars. And of course . . . ferries also had bars.

My father had always said that I could visit him whenever I wanted to, which I did at most once a year. Not that he ever visited me, that is.

Once there, I could try and tell him how miserable I had become. Not that he'd be able to fix it of course. He'd never been able to fix a single thing in my life. In fact, next to my mother, he was in large part responsible for me being the way I was, for he had left when I was very young, and I had been forced to live with my mother who had also neglected me throughout most of my life. Deciding between which of them was more responsible for my misery was like deciding between whether Fred or Rosemary West was more responsible for the nine people they killed.

Of course, no one was *ultimately* responsible. For anything. Free will was only an illusion and we were but puppets that couldn't see our strings. We thought that our choices were free only because evolution had built this illusion into us. In the end, however, both parents and serial killers had about as much freedom in their actions as a bullet exiting the barrel of a gun. And yet, I *still* blamed my parents. I had no choice not to.

But even if my father would end up being useless—which was likely—then perhaps I could at least find someone interesting to talk to on my little trip. Preferably someone with lines of worry on their face. Because I was about as tired of happy people as I was tired of breathing. And if not, then maybe at the very least I could meet some Finnish chick with whom I could finish what had been left unfinished with the tarot lady. Merely wishful thinking that, but I decided to buy the ticket anyway.

I didn't even bother calling my father to ask whether he was home; I just assumed he was. After I had bought the ticket through my phone and my fourth beer was empty, I left the bar. The ship to Helsinki went in about an hour.

The weather outside had turned rainy and windy. The ship I had bought the ticket for was a small catamaran, and there were bound to be lots of waves in the sea due to the wind. Not that it bothered me. Although I often became sick of things, I never became seasick.

After I arrived at the harbor, I walked under an awning, lit a Marlboro Red cigarette, and called my father to inform him of my imminent visit. The call started with the usual empty pleasantries.

"Hello," I said.

"Well hello there! How's it going?"

"It's . . . going. And you?"

"Oh, just like always."

I then asked him whether I could come and visit him in the evening. Sure, he said, adding that he was working right now but would be home later. When he asked me about the suddenness of my visit, I told him I was just going to be in the neighborhood. I didn't like to lie but I couldn't very well tell him that it was actually because I was depressed and needed a change of scenery. Like a million other fathers, he wasn't the kind of person you could talk to about your feelings.

Less than an hour later, the ferry sailed into the harbor and came to a stop at a nearby quay. The gangway was then lowered, on which the arriving passengers left the boat. Although there weren't many arriving or departing passengers, many of the departing passengers rushed towards it before the arriving passengers had even finished coming out, as if they might somehow get left behind. I waited until they had finished with their bustle.

After boarding, I headed straight for the bar. I bought a beer and a shot of whiskey and sat down by a window. I downed the whiskey immediately.

As the ship began to move, I watched the wavy sea from the window until the city lights faded into the distance. I then took out *Will O' the Wisp* and began reading:

Alain wanted to cry, waved goodnight, turned on his heel and ran down the stairs four at a time.

I was about halfway through the book when I saw the lights of Helsinki come into view from the ferry's window. I got up from my seat and walked to the outdoor deck on the back of the boat.

I lit a cigarette and looked around. Both the sky and water surrounding me were pitch black. It was as though the ferry was suspended in darkness. But then again, wasn't the entire planet?

18

WHEN I STEPPED OFF the ferry, it was drizzling rain. My father lived on the outskirts of Helsinki and the only way there that I knew of was by train.

I walked along the harbor promenade, then through the Esplanade Park, and finally through the city center, for about fifteen minutes, before reaching the entrance of the Helsinki Central Station, which was guarded by four towering Art Deco statues with somber faces, holding up spherical lamps.

The station was packed full of people as usual. I bought a ticket from the ticket machine, waited until the N-train arrived, and got on.

As the train started moving, I looked out the window and thought about my relationship with my father—or lack thereof. My father had a constant habit of letting me down, you see, of never doing what he said he would. For instance, he had told me he would give me a bunch of cash when I became an adult, to help me get started in life, which he never did. Then he told me he would give me his old Chrysler after he was going to buy a new one; instead, he sold it for peanuts. Once, going through some old documents, I discovered a life insurance policy in my name that he had signed up for; when I called the bank, however, it turned out he had cancelled it shortly after signing up.

The last time he had let me down was not so long ago. We were supposed to go to a rock concert together in Helsinki. It was my favorite band. As usual for him, he said sure, no problem. But when the day of the concert approached and I asked him about it, he suddenly said he wouldn't be able to make it. This was a constant theme with him. Not to mention the biggest letdown of them all—that he had disappeared for most of my fucking life.

Aside from that, he was also dismissive of my dreams. When I told him once that I wanted to become a writer, he laughed in my face and told me I that would never write anything. He was about as unmotivating as fathers got. The only suggestion he had given me when I had once gone to him because I was lost in life, was that I should sign up with the military "where they'd make a man out of me," which was about as stupid as it sounds.

Perhaps he was like that because he was just another gear in the machinery of life. A gear that never questioned the mechanisms around him, following them instead as if they were self-evident. How I had been begot by such a person was mystifying, but it seemed to confirm that the environment had a far greater effect on our personality than genes.

Since I had been deep in thought and it was dark outside, I missed my stop. I exited at the next station and walked through a graffiti-covered tunnel to the platform on the other side. It was very quiet and there was no one else around. I lit a Marlboro Red and waited for the train back.

Soon, a large group of Finnish teenagers walked onto the platform next to me. They were loud and drunk, passing a bottle of peppermint liqueur between them. I had the feeling that they might try and harass me, but fortunately they paid no attention to me, and the train soon arrived.

When I got off the train, I walked to a shop near my father's apartment. I bought a six-pack of beer and a small bottle of Jim Beam. The prices were twice as high as in Estonia. The whiskey was just in case I needed some help with falling asleep, as I often had trouble sleeping if I wasn't in my own bed. Not that I'd lately been able to fall asleep there either.

I slipped the whiskey into the inside pocket of my coat and grabbed the six-pack in my hand, trying to remember which of the bunch of identical apartment buildings he lived in.

I pressed the doorbell on one of the apartment buildings. "Kuka tuo on?" asked a raspy woman's voice. Wrong apartment. I tried another one. "Yes?" It was my father's voice. I told him it was me and he opened the door. I walked from the stairwell to the second floor and found the door with his name on it. I knocked once and the door opened.

"Well look who it is!" he said in a gentle voice. He

seemed genuinely happy to see me, perhaps also a little surprised considering how rarely I visited him.

"Hello," I said and stepped inside. "I brought some beer."

"Oh, I'm afraid you're gonna have to drink that all by yourself. I've got work early tomorrow."

I put down the beer. "How early?"

"Six o'clock."

"I see." I took off my coat and shoes. "Well, I'm used to drinking alone anyway." I wasn't sure whether he'd heard that last part. "By the way, if you're leaving so early, could you please drop me off at the harbor in the morning?"

"Sure, not a problem."

We walked into the living room which, as usual, was in a messy state. The TV was on, just like every other time I had visited him. Good old TV. The glue that held many a miserable life together. TV and work. You worked, you went home, you watched TV, and you went to sleep. Rinse and repeat.

"You hungry?" my father asked.

"As I last ate in the morning, I am indeed."

"Then help yourself to whatever's in the fridge. There's some eggs, bacon, potatoes, and bread in there."

"Thanks. Do you want any?"

"I've already eaten." He sat down and continued watching TV.

I went to the kitchen, opened one of the beers, put

the others in the fridge, and started fixing myself some food. So far so good.

After I was finished with the food, I walked to the living room with my plate and a new beer, sat down and started eating.

"So how are you?" he asked.

I decided to be honest for a change. "Not so good actually."

"Is that so? Well why not?"

"Where to start?" I took a sip of beer. "I hate my job. I don't have any friends. And to top it all off, my girlfriend of three years just left me. My life just hasn't turned out the way I wanted. None of my dreams have come true. In fact, I no longer seem to have any dreams. My life is just a constant and meaningless monotony where I'm doing the same thing over and over again, without any purpose."

He turned the volume down on the TV. "Well, then get a purpose! For instance, have a child."

I chuckled to myself. Ah yes, children. The perfect antidote for *my* misery. How little the bastard knew me. I wouldn't have wanted a child even if I was the last man on earth.

"There are just a few problems with that idea," I said. "First of all, I don't know if you heard me before, but my girlfriend just *left* me. Not that it matters since I don't like children anyway. Also, aren't there enough people in the world already? Do we really need to bring any more of them here? Without them having any choice in it either. People just capriciously keep forcing them into this world, especially when they're poor and unable to care for them. Not to mention that I can barely take care of myself, and I don't even like this world very much, so why the hell would I ever bring a child here?"

"Well, we've all thought that way once. But when you have a child, you'll change your mind."

"I can tell you with a hundred percent certainty that I will never bring a child into this fucked up world. That's one of the few things that I'm absolutely certain about. I'd rather hang myself."

He gave a long sigh. "You know, with that kind of attitude, you'll soon be a bitter old man, and no one will want to talk to you anymore."

"Guess what? I'm already bitter. And nobody already wants to talk to me."

"My god," he said, shaking his head. "What are we gonna do with you . . ."

"I would suggest abortion, but it's probably a little late for that."

"What?" he snapped. It looked like he didn't appreciate my dark humor.

"Well, it's just that the reason I'm here is because of you and mom. And I don't mean in this apartment, but in this world. This world that I don't like very much."

"Oh is that so?" I already knew where this was going. "You know, the problem with you is that you're too negative. Yes, there *are* problems in this world, but unless you have a solution, don't you dare criticize!"

I observed the vapid sitcom playing on the TV for a moment. "But I do have a solution."

"Oh you do, do you? And what is it?"

"It's simple. We've got to stop reproducing."

"Oh go away with such nonsense!" He waved his hand dismissively.

"How is that nonsense? All the problems in the world exist only because *we* exist. If there are no humans, there are no problems."

"But if there are no humans, then there's no point to anything."

"There already isn't any."

"Oh is that so?" His tone had become mocking. "And how did you reach that conclusion?"

"By reading and thinking."

"Well, I don't know what kind of books you've been reading . . ."

"The philosophical kind."

"And *those* books told you *these* things you're telling me now?"

"Yes."

He shook his head. "Ah, son . . . I think you need to read different kinds of books."

"For example what? The Bible?"

"For example."

"Seriously?"

"Of course." He said it as if it was self-evident.

"There's lots of good advice in the Bible."

"For instance, how to be a gullible fool?"

He frowned. "*Have* you read it?"

"I tried, but I fell asleep. However, I *have* read The Satanic Bible, which was much better."

"Read it before you criticize it."

"In that case, perhaps you should read some of the books I've read before you criticize me? I'd like to see you try coming up with a counterargument against Benatar's asymmetry, for instance."

"Son, I don't need to read such nonsense."

"Or maybe you're just afraid to, because what I'm saying makes sense?"

To this he just shook his head once more and remained silent. He was probably at a loss for words. Questioning the value of life was taboo, after all, especially for previous generations, who believed that we should worship our parents, no matter how badly they raised us, and to adore life, even though being alive was shit most of the time.

In any case, I felt that he had no right to judge me. I read somewhere that the fathers of many philosophers, including Nietzsche's, had either died or abandoned their children early on, which would explain why they began questioning everything from an early age because they did not have an authoritative father figure to give structure to their lives. If this was true, it was possible that it was largely because of him that I was the way I was and no longer believed in anything.

After finishing my meal, I opened a new beer and sat in silence for a while, watching the idiotic sitcom playing on the TV, in which I could not find a single humorous element. Like most sitcoms, it revolved around family, a concept completely alien to me. Moreover, it came with a laugh track, as though people were so goddamn stupid they even had to be told when to laugh.

Noticing how quickly I poured the beer down my throat, my father suddenly opened his mouth and said, "And I see you've become an alcoholic as well!"

"I just like the taste."

"But you're already an alcoholic if you like the taste!"

I took a big sip of beer. "Is that so?"

"A normal person drinks when there's something to celebrate," he explained in his endless wisdom. "If you're just drinking by yourself, you're already an alcoholic."

"If you say so." I suddenly recalled an image from my childhood where I'd been at a party with him where he had gotten shit-faced and then fell asleep on a random bed. Being around five or six years old at the time and not knowing what I should do at a party full of drunk strangers, I went to him and tried to shake him awake, but all he said was, "Fuck off," before shoving me away.

"So how's your mother doing?" he suddenly asked. He always asked the same questions.

"All right, I guess. We don't talk much."

"Why not?"

"Because I don't see her that often."

"I see. And what happened with your girlfriend?"

"She left me. That's what happened."

"Well, if she had to listen to the same things I just had to listen to, then I'm not surprised." My father, sensitive as always.

We sat on the couch and continued watching TV. It was clear that coming there had been a mistake. I'd have gotten about as much "understanding" from a stranger at a bar as from my own father. Talking with him was futile. We had nothing in common. And he was of no help whatsoever for my current mental state. How could such a dissimilar person be my father, I wondered? Once again, environment one, genes zero.

"Well, I'm off to bed," he eventually said, getting up from the couch, as if our conversation just now hadn't even happened. "The alarm is set at five in the morning. Good night." He left the room.

I finished my beers, watching the entertainment on TV which failed to entertain me. And then I opened the whiskey.

19

I WOKE UP IN the morning due to the noise my father was making whilst getting ready for work. I was slightly hungover.

Once we were ready, we went downstairs and walked to his car. He seemed to have a different car every time I visited him. Perhaps it had something to do with his love of poker. This time he had an old van. When I asked him why he was driving around in a van, he said he just liked to in case he needed to transport anything. I looked at the back of the van; it was empty.

We started driving. It was still dark outside, and the streets were empty. After driving for around twenty minutes whilst listening to bad rock songs on the radio, we finally arrived at the harbor. He stopped the car in front of the terminal building.

"Listen, I'm sorry to hear that you're not doing well," he said. "But I hope you manage to solve your problems somehow. Remember that you can always visit or call if you need anything."

Anything but understanding.

"All right," I said, opening the van door. "Good-bye."

He waved at me as he drove off. I didn't wave back.

I walked inside the terminal building and went to the ticket office. I bought a ticket for the next ship to Tallinn, which was due in about an hour.

Then I went back out and lit a cigarette. It was beginning to get light outside. I walked to the pier and watched the waves of the Baltic Sea. I had always liked the sea. Right now, I would have liked to have drowned in it.

After I had finished my second cigarette, I went back inside. I sat down on a bench, took out *Will O' the Wisp* and started reading:

"Yes, that's true, he is very unhappy," Praline went on. "It will all come to a bad end . . . but he won't kill himself."

"How do you know?" hissed Totote.

I read it slowly, deliberately, making sure my mind recorded every sentence, every word. After all, it might end up being the last book that I would ever read.

When I was about two-thirds through, I put the book away. It was time to get on the ship. I walked through the gate, scanned my ticket, and walked on board. The ship was much bigger than the one I had taken to Helsinki.

The first thing I did was go to the bar. It was early as shit for a beer, but I didn't care. It was getting harder and harder to care about anything at this point, especially myself.

I sat down behind the counter and ordered a beer. Next to me sat a brunette lady who, despite her heavy makeup, seemed to be in her late thirties or early forties. There was a gin and tonic in front of her. Despite the early hour, she already seemed to be drunk.

I took a sip from my beer. "Hello there," I said, "fellow alcoholic."

"Who? Me?" She raised her eyebrows. "I've just been on a night out with my girlfriends. I actually live in Tallinn."

"You were out on a Monday night?"

"Well, you see . . . the night out *started* on Saturday."

"I see. Your stamina is quite impressive. But Helsinki is kind of a long way to go for a night out, isn't it?"

"Yes, well, even though I live in Tallinn, I'm actually Finnish and most of my friends live in Finland."

"Ah, I see." I took a big sip of beer.

"And you? What are you doing here at such an early hour?"

"Just trying to find an attractive drunk Finnish woman, that's all."

She laughed. "Do you wanna do some tequila shots with me?"

"Sure. Why not."

She bought the shots. The bartender looked at us a little funny, but nevertheless served us our drinks, before moving on to serve some fat Finnish fuck with a gut as big as a priest's.

We downed the tequilas. She put her hand on my leg. Déjà vu.

"Wanna come to my cabin?"

"To, uh, read the Bible together?"

"Ei tietenkään. To fuck."

I quickly poured what was left of my beer down my throat and said, "Let's go."

We got up from our seats. As we walked to her cabin, I had to support her here and there so she wouldn't fall over. Some of the people we passed by stared at us, but I didn't care. The woman had clearly been drinking a *lot* and had probably barely slept. We got lost a few times in the identical-looking labyrinthine corridors until we finally found the right cabin. She fumbled with the keycard a little before getting the door open.

As soon as we had entered the cabin and closed the door, she was already on her knees and started unbuttoning my pants. She took my cock in her mouth like a hungry animal and started sucking on it ferociously. I wasn't sure whether she was a nymphomaniac or just hadn't had sex in a while.

She sucked me for a few minutes before she went over to the bed and pulled down her tights. I stepped over to her and put some saliva on my penis. She moaned as I slid it into her.

After a few minutes of fucking, she said, "I want you to put it in my ass."

My god. This lady is a freak.

I did as she requested. It was much tighter in there. I pumped away at her ass for a while until I was ready to come. "I'm coming," I announced, but there was no response. A few more strokes and I came inside.

I took my penis out and wiped it clean against the bedding. She was laying still. I examined her face and noticed she was slightly snoring. She had fallen asleep whilst I had been fucking her. I was beginning to think that the only way someone was able to tolerate me was when they were dead drunk. At the same time, I was also only able to tolerate most people when I was drunk as fuck myself. Was that what they meant by symbiosis?

I considered the situation I was in. I was in her cabin whilst she slept. I knew there was no way I could have woken her, even if I had wanted to, because she was practically in a coma. So my only option was to leave the cabin. I was pretty sure she was still going to be passed out when we arrived in the harbor, meaning that one of the ship's cleaners would probably find her, that bare ass towards her, my sperm oozing out of it.

I tried to pull up her tights, but it was futile in the position she was in. I also didn't want to wait for another hour in the cabin until the ship arrived in port, because I was sure that if she woke up, she wouldn't remember me and would no doubt be surprised to find herself naked in her cabin with a stranger. Therefore, my only option was to leave her there like some rape victim.

I paused before exiting the cabin and looked at her bare ass visible from the doorway. "Goodbye," I said to the ass and left.

It felt a bit strange walking down the hallway, as though I had just done something criminal. But on the plus side, I had indeed fucked a Finnish lady, just as I had wanted to, even if it had been a somewhat pitiable affair. On the other hand, the main reason for the trip had gone as I had subconsciously expected it to go. Still, the experience I'd just had was a kind of silver lining—albeit in a storm cloud—and had invigorated me somewhat. If these were to be my last days on earth, I thought, I could at least *try* to spend them by enjoying myself, as little as I was capable of that these days.

I headed to the duty-free shop to buy some liquor. Since they had a good deal on Jack Daniel's, I bought a liter of it. I also bought one of those tiny liquor bottles—this one had a blue liquid in it and was shaped like a ship—as well as a tuna sandwich and a beer. After I got my items, I walked outside to the sundeck where there was no sun.

I sat down in a secluded spot, unwrapped the sandwich, and sipped on the beer whilst watching the sea. It was a gray and foggy day. The air smelled good. There was nobody else on the deck that I could see.

After I was done with the sandwich and beer, I lit a Marlboro Red. I heard somewhere that a cigarette took ten minutes from your life. But so did ten minutes of talking about the weather. I opened the small bottle of blue alcohol and poured it down my throat, but it did next to nothing for me. I didn't want to open the Jack Daniel's yet because it was a big bottle and I wasn't yet quite on the same level of not giving a fuck as, say, Billy Bob Thornton's character in *Bad Santa*. Then I remembered the smaller bottle of whiskey I had in my coat pocket from the day before. It was half full. Or was it half empty? Hmm. I opened it and took a sip.

I used to not like whiskey. In fact, its taste had made me want to vomit. But one day after something really bad had happened to me, the first thing I did was to go out and buy a big bottle of whiskey. And on that day, for some reason, it started to taste pretty good to me. I guess my brain must have been too busy with the pain I was in at the time, so it had ignored the bitter taste. And when the pain had finally subsided—had it?—I was already used to the bitterness.

After sitting on the deck for a while and watching the waves, I finally saw land in the distance. The ship was going to arrive soon. I finished the whiskey just as the ship was nearing the shore. Since I couldn't see anyone else on the deck, I flung the bottle overboard as hard as I could. Perhaps an alcoholic fish could make a home of it.

I left the deck and started walking towards the exit, thinking about what I was going to do next in my meaningless life. Whatever it was, I knew it would involve drinking. The question was whether I'd be drinking alone or with other people.

It was a choice that hardly mattered as I was bound to end up disappointed in either way.

20

AFTER I GOT BACK on solid ground, I first headed home. I cleaned up the shards of glass from the whiskey bottle and located an old flask which had the quote, "Find what you love and let it kill you," engraved on it. It was supposed to be a quote from Bukowski, but it turned out to have been misattributed. Of course, since the flask was a gift from an ex-girlfriend, it might as well have said, "Find what you love and let it leave you." I filled it with the Jack Daniel's.

I went to the bathroom to finally remove the homemade bandage on my foot. The wound looked quite nasty, but it didn't hurt. I then took a shower. When the hot water fell on me, I thought about what I could possibly love enough in this world to let it kill me. I concluded that it could only be one of three things—a woman, alcohol, or a gun.

When I was all done, I decided to leave the apartment. I had no destination in mind; I just had to get out of there. For there were still far too many shadows there, far too many memories, far too much pain. And being there in the daytime was even worse than being there in the evening because in the evening I tended to see everything through an alcoholic haze, which made reality seem less real somehow and therefore more tolerable.

I walked to the bus stop. Whilst on the bus, I noticed a woman who reminded me of the first woman I'd had intercourse with after Vicky had left me. It had been a Russian escort. During one drunk and desperate night, I had surfed escort websites and had chosen one that had seemed attractive enough—at least on pictures—as well as not too expensive (for some reason, Russian escorts were the cheapest) and had sent her a message. I had already forgotten about it the next day when I suddenly received a response. I met her the day after. To calm my nerves, I had gotten a little drunk beforehand.

The escort didn't quite look like she had on the internet. She was at least ten years older, and her photos had clearly been heavily processed. But beggars can't be choosers. Worse, I had to speak to her in bad English because she did not speak any Estonian and I did not speak any Russian. It made our intercourse rather awkward. She initially gave me a blowjob without a condom and then put a condom on me and leaned on the bed. My penis was only half hard, but I pushed it in. While the blowjob had still felt partially enjoyable, the condom removed any pleasure I might have had. Her cold demeanor, which was to be expected, didn't help either. We tried a few different positions, but I could never get a complete hard-on. In the end, I had to resign myself to masturbating until I came on her stomach, my semen flowing onto her cesarean scar.

No doubt it had been a rather pitiful intercourse with a sad connotation. It was unfortunate that there were women in this world who had no choice but to work at such distasteful jobs to survive. Of course, we all sold our bodies. Some of us our muscles. Some of us our brains. And some of us our holes. In the end, we had no choice but to sell ourselves. We were slaves.

I'd always had a rather big sex drive. That had been one of the many reasons Vicky had left me. She wanted to have sex once a week; I wanted it every day. And despite my recent sexual escapade on the ship—or perhaps because of it—I still felt somewhat horny. That's why when I arrived in the city center, I decided to go to the sex shop with porn booths on Tatari street, which I had visited once before out of interest without actually doing anything in there.

I knew that the probability of meeting women in such a sleazy place was virtually zero. But that wasn't the point. So what was the point? I didn't know. What was the point of anything? Did it matter if we did one thing or another? And if so, where was it written in the universe? And even if it was written somewhere, how would we know that it wasn't just something that someone had made up? We couldn't. So it didn't matter what we did. Nothing mattered. And thus, I went to the sex shop.

When I arrived, I first browsed the dildos and porn

movies for a while, while the woman behind the counter was dealing with a customer. After the customer had received his artificial vagina and left, I paid the lady behind the counter an entrance fee and bought a beer (yes, they sold beer there).

I then walked through the beaded curtain-covered doorway with the beer in my hand. Right away, a strong smell of sperm wafted into my nostrils. In front of me were red and purple corridors and small rooms with video screens where a variety of pornography was being played. There was also a small hall with a slightly bigger screen. For obvious reasons, it was also quite dark in there.

As far as I knew, most people who went to porn cinemas were homosexuals hoping to meet other homosexuals. And as far as I knew, I wasn't a homosexual. Even though I sometimes got turned on when looking at erect penises.

I looked around the different rooms to see what kind of porn was playing inside them, until I reached a small room where an old man with a Santa Claus beard was jerking off. I was taken aback as I hadn't expected to find anyone in there. He turned around and gave me a mischievous smile, motioning towards his wrinkled cock with his hungry eyes.

I quickly closed the door and stepped into the first porn booth I saw, locking the door behind me. I waited there quietly for a while until I was sure I couldn't hear anybody outside. I then sat down and started watched the porn playing on the screen whilst sipping on my beer until I got an erection. I took out my cock and started rubbing it. The porn that was playing was an interracial gangbang; five black men were fucking a blonde white girl with big tits. She had one cock in her ass, one in her vagina, one in her mouth, and at the same time she was jerking off the two other guys. For whichever reason, I preferred gangbang porn the most.

I watched the porn until all the men came on the woman's face. I timed it so that I came at the same time. Then I finished my beer and left. The experience left me cold. It was better to masturbate at home, I thought.

On the street, I bought a pack of cigarettes from a nearby kiosk. I wasn't in the mood to go to a bar yet, so for a change I decided to go to a regular cinema instead, where at least I wouldn't have to meet any wrinkled old fags . . . probably.

Since I didn't like having lots of people around, and I didn't like mainstream movies, I chose an arthouse cinema. Not that I necessarily liked those either. There were only two such cinemas in Tallinn and I chose the one that was closer to me.

When I got there, I learned that a movie would start in about fifteen minutes. It was a French film called *La Vie des morts*. I generally didn't like French films because they were often dull and pretentious, but what the hell. I bought a ticket and a bottle of beer and stepped into the small auditorium. There were only two other people there, two women. I took a seat in the middle of the back row.

The film began shortly. At the beginning of it, a young man was in a coma at a hospital after a botched suicide attempt. I couldn't help but wonder how successful I'd be in committing suicide, given that I hadn't exactly been successful with anything else in life. If I were to do it—or more precisely *when* I were to do it—I would probably do so by hanging myself from the metal beam in the wardrobe of my apartment; it was high enough and looked quite sturdy, almost as if it was designed for this. Of course, I couldn't guarantee that it wouldn't break or that I wouldn't have any second doubts.

I tried to focus on the film, but the conversation between the two women in the auditorium became more and more loud. It was as if they had come to the cinema just to talk to each other, instead of watching the movie. Couldn't they have done that it in a cafe instead? What the fuck was wrong with people?

Finally, when I couldn't stand it any longer, I said in a loud voice, "Hey! Yeah, you two. Could you please shut the fuck up?"

They flashed me some dirty looks and kept on talking more quietly.

Although the film had seemed interesting at first, by the end of it I felt that it was nothing special; it had focused far too much on the family of the victim and, as usual, it ended with a positive note, which I abhorred. Did anything in life ever end on a positive note? In fact, did life? Although death wasn't necessarily a bad thing, you lost everything you ever had when you died, everything you ever lived for. So what was the point of it all? Why not skip this pointless and drawn-out episode between birth and death altogether?

When I left the cinema, I saw the two women again. "What's your problem?" one of them asked as I walked past her.

"Inconsideration," I said without stopping. It was the same problem I had against the universe.

21

AFTER LUNCH, WHICH CONSISTED of greasy noodles and a Tsingtao beer at a Chinese fast-food joint, I walked around the city smoking cigarettes.

I ended up in Rotermann Quarter, its old limestone factory buildings contrasting the new glass and metal architecture. I had gone there because I had once stumbled upon a strange bar there called Disremember—a very apt name for a bar. Its colorful and contrasting interior design had consisted of Russian icons and modern art, and as far as I could remember, I had met some interesting patrons there.

The reason I was looking for this bar was because I was still on my never-ending quest to find someone worth talking to, someone who had something interesting to say, someone who'd listen, someone who'd understand. Even as all I had found so far were NPCs who were about as fake as Pamela Anderson's tits and who immediately lost interest in me the minute I started talking about my views. Views which, after all, were perfectly reasonable, if not a little bleak. But then so was life. I couldn't help it. I didn't make it. I wouldn't have wanted to. If a God made this world, as Schopenhauer said, then I would not want to be its

God, for its misery and despair would break my heart.

However, when I got to the place where the bar was supposed to be, there was nothing there. I was *sure* there had been a bar there. I even circled around it, making sure I didn't disremember where it was supposed to be, but it could only have been in one place and on that spot was nothing but a paved square with no sign that there had ever been a bar there.

I lit a cigarette. Strange, I thought. Very strange.

For lack of any better ideas, I decided to head to Scarlet Emperor again, which was nearby. Whilst walking there, the sun came out for a change. Not that I cared about that; in fact, I would have preferred if it had rained.

The walk took me through Kanuti Garden, where a monument to Dostoevsky stood. His *Notes from the Underground* was one of the finest books I had ever read on account of its stark and honest portrayal of alienation, suffering, and human pettiness. I paused before the monument; it was covered in bird shit. Even when you're dead, they still shit on you.

Although all sorts of odd people could often be found in Scarlet Emperor, when I arrived there, I saw that it was practically empty. This was probably not surprising, given that it was Tuesday.

Behind the counter stood the same goth barmaid as the last time. I ordered a house beer. "It's very empty here," I said after she finished pouring my drink.

"It's too early," she said.

"And yet, I'm here."

"Yes." She squinted her eyes. "Why are you?"

"Because my father didn't wear a condom."

"I meant here in this bar."

"Because much like Diogenes, I am looking for a human being. Unfortunately, I've yet to find any."

Her eyebrows rose. "Okay . . ."

I figured she wasn't going to make a very good conversation partner, so I smiled at her awkwardly and walked away from the counter. I sat behind an empty table and focused on my beer.

Come to think of it, I couldn't recall having ever met a goth with a personality. I guess what they lacked in personality they tried to make up with in appearance since otherwise nobody would find them attractive. And she *was* attractive . . . though ultimately little more than the dark version of a bimbo.

Still, I would have liked to have fucked her. My cock was getting hard just thinking about it. I looked around; there was no one there. Inspired by Dan Fante, I unzipped my pants and took out my cock. I began stroking it, fantasizing about fucking the goth in the ass. After a few minutes, I shot my load into a napkin. I wiped myself clean and put it away. No one had seen me.

After I had polished off my beer, I considered what I was going to do next. I could finish reading *Will o' the Wisp*, I thought. I still had about one third of it left. But I didn't want to do it in this bar; for some reason, its atmosphere without people in it was strangely depressing. I also didn't want to go home yet. Since the sun was out and it wasn't very cold outside, I decided to go to a park instead. I could even buy some beers and sip on them whilst sitting on a park bench. The plan seemed sound.

Before leaving the bar, I went to the counter and told the barmaid to give me a shot.

"What kind?"

"Nine millimeters."

22

AFTER I HAD BOUGHT a six-pack of Heineken from a nearby shop, I went to Freedom Square. I climbed the steps until I reached the top of Harjumäe Park, where there was a small pavilion, a fountain, and benches. Near one of the benches stood a few teenagers listening to shitty techno music from their phone and drinking cider. They looked underage.

I chose a bench away from them. I put my beers on the bench and sat down. In front of me was a nice view overlooking Freedom Square, with high-rise buildings in the distance. On the square was a row of Estonian flags and a ridiculously expensive monument commemorating the Estonian War of Independence.

There was also the church where my aunt's funeral had been held. I remembered standing over her open casket, looking at her lifeless body, feeling the stench of decay. She had looked so peaceful. Although it was a great tragedy for the people at the funeral that she was gone, some of them even openly weeping over her, in truth, death was only a tragedy to those left behind. For my aunt, all her troubles were over. For the people weeping over her, something valuable had been taken from their lives without their consent. Their tears were born from selfishness.

I cracked open a beer and took out *Will o' the Wisp*. I took a sip and started reading:

Why was Alain going on? Had he not seen enough? And if he wanted to kill himself, what better time was there than seven or eight o'clock in the evening, when all the passions, unburdened from work, rush at full speed across town in a maddening vortex? But no, life is only a habit, and the habit holds you as long as life lasts.

I read for about an hour, consuming three beers in the process, until finally I arrived at the last sentence: "To die is the finest thing you could do, the most positive, the most you could do."

As I closed the book, I felt as if someone had stuck a dagger in my heart. My eyes got wet. I sat on the bench for a long time, looking into the distance, thinking about Alain's bleak ending, wondering whether mine would end up being the same.

After I had recovered somewhat, I lit a cigarette. Soon afterwards a man who looked like a homeless person approached my bench. He had a bushy beard, curly hair, and he was wearing an old black suit which was somewhat dirty.

"I didn't want to bother you before because you was reading," he said.

I blew a puff of smoke out of my mouth. "That's all

right."

"What were you reading, by the way?"

"Well . . ." I took a deep breath. "It's basically a book about a guy who's very unhappy. And he's trying to find a reason to stay alive. But he can't find any."

"Sounds like heavy stuff. Why were you reading it?"

"Because it reminds me of my own life."

He nodded. "Yeah, this world's a cruel place all right, no doubt about that." He pointed towards himself. "Believe me, I know."

"I bet you do."

"By the way, I see you're drinking beer. Would you mind offering me one, by any chance?"

"Not at all," I said, handing him a can of Heineken and taking a new one for myself.

"Many thanks."

He sat down next to me, opened the can, and took a big gulp. "That goes down real smooth," he said.

We sat there for a while and drank our beers.

"By the way," I said. "I also have some whiskey if you're interested." I took out the flask and shook it.

"Say, that's a very nice flask you got there. What's it say?"

I turned it in my hand, letting the sunlight glint off the engraved words. "It says, find what you love and let it kill you."

He wrinkled his brow. "And what does that mean?"

I thought for a moment. "I guess it means that since we're all going to die anyway, it's best to die doing something we love."

"Like . . . drinking, for instance?"

"Yes. Or chasing girls."

He flashed a toothy grin—a few teeth were missing—and chuckled. "Ain't that the truth."

I uncorked the flask and extended it to him.

"Wait. I know you don't want to share it with an old bum like me. We'll drink it like proper gentlemen." He put his hand in his pocket and brought out something that was wrapped in a paper towel. He unwrapped it; inside were two shot glasses. "Don't worry, they's clean. I got them from a bar. They've just been waiting for the right time." He handed me one of the glasses.

"Thanks," I said and poured us both a shot.

"Much obliged."

I began lifting the glass to my mouth when he suddenly said, "Wait, wait. We need a toast."

"A toast?"

"Yessir. Proper."

"All right. Do you have one?"

He thought for a moment. "To strangers . . . who are kind with their liquor!"

"To kind strangers!"

After we downed our shots, I poured us both a new one.

"Okay, I have one too," I said.

"I'm listening."

"To surviving . . . in a world that doesn't give a

shit!"

He nodded. "Hey, that's pretty good."

We downed the shots.

Afterwards, I offered him a cigarette. We then sat there for a while, smoking cigarettes, and looking at the skyline. The sun was beginning to set, drowning everything in a blood-red hue. One day the sun would be no more. Nothing would.

After a while, my companion opened his mouth. "As I said, I know. I know this world ain't worth to piss on. I know most people be crooked. Even bums be stealing from me from time to time. Not that I've anything worth stealing." He chuckled. "Yeah, I've even put my head on them railroad tracks a few times, waiting for the train to arrive. But every time I start seeing that train in the distance, I think, well . . . maybe I should just wait a bit, you know? Maybe it's gonna get a little better. Maybe not a whole lot, but maybe it'll be enough."

"And? Has it gotten any better?"

"I suppose so. Seeing as I'm still alive."

I sighed. "It only seems to be getting worse for me."

"Or maybe you just haven't gotten to that point yet where you're ready to lay your head on them railroad tracks. Maybe when you do, you'll wanna wait just a little longer. See what the future brings. Maybe it brings a little something, you know? Cause ain't like you've got anything left to lose at that point."

I considered what he said for a moment. "Yeah, I

guess you've got a point."

He pulled up one of his sleeves and looked at the time; it didn't seem as though the watch was working. "Well, I gotta get going soon."

"One more shot before you go?"

"Of course. If you're offering."

I filled our glasses. The flask was empty now.

"Awfully kind of you."

We downed the shots.

"Do you have a place to go?" I asked.

"Well, there's always a place to go. Problem is where to stay."

"Yeah, I guess that's the problem all right." I handed him the empty shot glass.

"Keep it," he said.

"You sure?"

"Yes. Ain't nothing for me to do with two. And try to steer clear from them railroad tracks, you hear?"

"Thanks. I'll try."

He got up from the bench. "Well, good luck to you."

"To you as well."

He started walking away.

I sipped on my last beer and watched the sunset. Perhaps Alain should have also just waited a little while longer? Or perhaps he had already waited long enough.

I sat there until the last rays of the sun were gone and the sky was dark. It seemed like I had finally met a human being. And talking with him had almost given me hope that things might get better. Almost . . . but not quite.

I suddenly felt exhausted. I had slept very little during the last few days. I decided to take the next bus home. Tomorrow was another day.

23

I SLEPT FOR AT least ten hours that night. Before getting up, I reread Akutagawa's short story *The Life of a Stupid Man*, which ended with the sentence: "He barely made it through each day in the gloom, leaning as it were upon a chipped and narrow sword." Akutagawa had written it shortly before his suicide. And thus, it ended with defeat. As did his life. As did everything in the end.

Still, my mood was a little better than it had been during the last couple of days. Not that it was good, mind you; it hadn't been good for a long fucking time now. But it was manageable.

After I got up and took a shower, I decided to cook myself some breakfast for a change. I walked to the nearby Russian store and bought some bacon, eggs, toast, and orange juice. When I got home, I washed some of the moldy dishes in the sink, almost throwing up in the process.

Once I had finished eating, I made coffee and put on some music. Then I took a random book out of my bookshelf and tried reading it, but I couldn't concentrate on it long enough. Instead, I watched porn and masturbated. In the end, however, I couldn't figure out what to do next. I didn't want to go to work, but I also didn't want to stay in the apartment.

I finally had no choice but to hit the town. Perhaps I could try finding my old drinking buddy Joe, I thought, and see how he was doing. If he was still alive, that is. I filled my flask with whiskey and sent him a text message.

It was four in the afternoon when I got on the bus. I still hadn't heard back from Joe, so I tried calling him, but his number wasn't active.

Once downtown, I headed to the main place Joe used to hang out in Old Town—a bar called Lowlander. Perhaps he'd be there; and if not, then perhaps the bartender would have some information about his whereabouts.

There was a Scottish flag waving outside the bar and the steps led underground. I descended the steps and entered. Inside was a rather small and ancient-looking room with old stone walls and floors. The ceiling was covered in tartan fabric and the walls were decorated with swords and axes. On one wall hung the soulless-looking head of a taxidermy deer.

I walked to the small bar counter and sat down on a bar stool. The bartender had long hair and a beard and was wearing a kilt; I wondered whether he was naked under it. I ordered a beer. After he had finished pouring it, I asked him whether he'd seen Joe by any chance.

He thought for a moment. "Come to think of it, I

haven't."

"As far as I know, he used to come here almost every night."

"That's true, yeah. He practically lived here. But then he suddenly stopped coming. I haven't seen him in months."

"I see. Thanks for the information."

Joe had a heart condition; it was something he had been born with. He had told me it would end up killing him one day. And his massive drinking certainly didn't do him any good in that regard. Of course, there was also another possibility—suicide. We had talked about it a few times. The best way to do it, when to do it, how it would affect the ones left behind and so on. Could he have been hanging from a ceiling somewhere, I wondered? It was possible. Or given what a drunkard he was, he could have also just been in some sort of accident; it wouldn't have been the first time. It was hard to know exactly what could have happened to him.

All I knew was that one thing was utterly impossible—that he had stopped drinking.

24

FINISHED WITH MY BEER, I left the bar. I walked aimlessly around Old Town for a while, observing all the seemingly happy people passing me by. Yet behind their smiles were skulls. They were the walking dead. It was only a matter of time.

As I was walking up a cobblestone street towards Toompea Castle, I noticed a painter selling his works by the roadside. I couldn't help but feel sorry for him. In this world they put a price tag on everything, including art. And if it didn't sell, it was deemed worthless, regardless of its actual worth. This was contrary to the principle of art—real art was individual, novel, and bold. But because its value in our world was proportional to its popularity, it had to aim for the lowest common denominator, which was so low that it couldn't possibly be considered art anymore.

Of course, this tended to apply more to other forms of art such as films and novels and music. No, the world of paintings was even stranger. It was a world of filthy rich people who bought paintings of a couple of cubes for a hundred million dollars. Yeah, try explaining the logic behind *that* to an extra-terrestrial who has just landed on Earth.

Having walked past a giant Russian Orthodox church with golden crosses and icons adorning it, I saw that a big crowd had gathered on the square in front of the pink Baroque Parliament building. It seemed to be a demonstration of some sort.

As I walked closer, I saw people holding up signs saying, "Become vegan," "Stop killing animals," "Save the planet," "Go green," and so on. I also saw a sign with a photo of a calf which said, "I want to live," as well as a sign with a photo of a piglet which said, "Being vegan saves lives." I noticed that most of the protesters were slender young women, though there were also some families and children.

As I was walking past them, a girl with green hair and a nose piercing—a typical sign of her tribe—came up to me and asked me if I wanted to sign her petition. As if petitions had ever changed a single thing in this fucking world. Nevertheless, I decided to humor her.

"What's it about?"

"It's about how innocent animals don't need to suffer and die just because some people like the taste of meat."

"What about people? Do people have to suffer and die?"

"This is about animals, not people."

"But why not? A human being is just another animal. An animal that, by the way, suffers far more than any other animal because he alone knows that he will die and that all of his suffering is ultimately futile."

"I'm afraid I couldn't care less about humans when they commit genocide against animals just because they can't control their urge to eat meat or wear leather."

"Then I'm afraid I simply don't care enough about animals not to eat their meat." I eyed both of our leather shoes. "Or to not wear leather."

She snorted. "You don't care about animals? Okay. But do you care about the planet? Did you know that eating meat causes global warming?"

"So?"

"So raising animals in order to eat their meat is a huge contributor of greenhouse gases into the atmosphere. And if we want to stop global warming, we need to start eating less meat, ideally none."

"All right. But driving a car—including an electric one—or flying in an airplane emits far more greenhouse gases than eating meat. So should we also stop driving cars or flying airplanes?"

"That's another matter."

"All right. But what about children?"

"What about them?"

"Don't you think we should have less children, ideally none?"

"Of course not. Why would I think that?"

"Because if there are no people, then no one would be killing and eating the animals, except, of course, other animals. There'd also be no global warming, except, of course, the kind that happens naturally without people. There'd be no pollution, except, again, the natural kind. And finally, there would be no destruction of animal habitats, at least not through humans. So not having children is, logically speaking, the greenest thing you can ever do for animals and nature."

"That may be. But we can't just force people to stop having children."

"But we can force them to stop eating meat? Even though we've been eating it for millions of years?"

"We're not trying to force anyone; we're just trying to persuade them." As she said this, demonstrators were shouting in the background: "An animal has feelings, a meat eater has none!"

"Well, then you're not doing a very good job at it. It looks more like you're trying to shame people. Which would be all right as long as you shamed them for something more worthwhile. For instance—that they constantly keep forcing more and more people into this world who haven't asked to be born. People that will suffer, cause others to suffer, eat animals, pollute, waste resources, and so on. Did you know that in the last fifty years, when the human population has doubled, more than half of the world's wild animals have become extinct? And not because we *ate* them, but simply because there are too many fucking people on this planet and the idiots keep making even more!"

"Listen," she waved her finger in front of my face, "no privileged white male is going to tell *me* what I can or cannot do with *my* body. If *I* want to have a child, then that's *my* choice. And if that child becomes a vegan, that's also my choice."

Me, me, me. You selfish bitch.

"And eating meat is *my* choice."

"Unfortunately, yes. But you can't compare having a child to slaughtering thousands of animals for their meat!"

"As though *I'm* doing the slaughtering."

"Still, the end result is the same."

I was tired of talking with her. She obviously wasn't listening, and probably didn't even want to listen. But I couldn't let her have the last word, especially one as lousy as that. It just wasn't in my nature.

"Have you ever heard of an organization called Church of Euthanasia?"

She crossed her arms. "Can't say that I have."

"Well, they're not very active anymore, but they also used to be very worried about the planet. However, *their* slogan was, 'Save the planet, kill yourself.' And if you guys looked at it all from a slightly bigger perspective, you'd advocate the same. In fact, if you wanted to be *especially* green, what you should do is commit mass suicide, just like in Jonestown in the seventies. And best of all, afterwards you could have the animals eat your bodies."

With each word that I had said, she seemed to have gotten more and more triggered. "I . . . just CAN'T!" She gritted her teeth. "Why . . . would you say something like THAT? ARGH!" She stormed away.

I guess my work here was done. I lit a cigarette and started walking away. I had nothing against vegans, you see, but what I couldn't stand were hypocrites. Not that her reaction had been unusual of course. Antinatalism—the idea that we should stop reproducing—was not a very popular idea, not even amongst green freaks. This despite the fact that all of the troubles in the world existed only because *we* existed, and that bringing more children into this world, as Zapffe put it, was like carrying wood to a burning house.

Despite the obviousness of this idea, talking to the average person about it was like confessing to a murder. That's because even in a post-apocalyptic wasteland—which our planet would inevitably become—where all that existed was misery and squalor, people, in their never-ending capacity for self-delusion, would still go on bringing new beings into this world. So strongly had the idea that existence was preferable to non-existence been implanted into us. It *had* to be because otherwise there wouldn't be any humans around.

Life was like a pyramid scheme that had to be constantly pushed down the throats of new victims in order to keep the scam going.

25

BY THE TIME I had walked back down from Toompea, I had developed a craving for some steak. Good steak. Not like the one I'd had with Vicky. And while walking on Rüütli street, I noticed a restaurant called Purgatorium, which seemed like the kind of place that might serve good steak. The restaurant was underground, in a very old building with white and red arched ceilings and heavy wrought iron chairs and tables.

After I sat down at a table, a fat waitress brought me the menu. I flicked through it and chose the most expensive item on it; my bank account be damned. It was a steak with oven-baked vegetables and a port sauce. When the waitress came back to take my order, I asked her how much fat it had; she said none, so I ordered it. I also ordered a smoked lager with an alcohol content of six point sixty-six percent.

She left for a moment and came back with the beer. I had a taste. It was disgusting. One of the worst beers I had ever drank; it tasted like it was rotten. Why the hell did people like these disgusting craft beers so much?

While waiting for my steak, I examined the painting hanging on the wall next to me. It was an abstract that consisted entirely of textured black smudges. Was there a meaning to the black smudges? Perhaps. Or perhaps it was like a Rorschach test and the meaning came from inside our own brains. If so, all I could see in it were the suffering slaves of hell, wriggling like worms in their miserable struggle.

Eventually the waitress brought me my steak. I cut a piece of the meat and put it in my mouth. The first thing I tasted was fat; the steak was full of it. Then I tried the vegetables, which weren't cooked through properly. This had been the most expensive item on the menu . . . and it fucking sucked. Apparently, even the good things in this world sucked. Why was it so hard to find a decent steak? Why was there so much fat on everything—I looked towards the waitress— especially on the people?

After I was finished with the meal, the waitress came to take away my plate. She asked me how I had liked it. I pointed at all the fat left on the plate and politely told her what I thought of it. She said she'd let the kitchen know, which was probably a lie and didn't really help me in any way. Besides, *she* had been the one who had told me that there was no fat in it.

Well, that's how it was in this world. My steak was like a microcosm of how everything was always sold to us as an ideal, even though in reality it was only half of that at best or less. Yet most of us did not complain because we were so used to lying, both to ourselves and to others, that everything was fine all the time. We lied to others because we were cowards who didn't want to rock the boat, and we lied to ourselves because we didn't dare to admit that we were being lied to wherever we went.

Or ... perhaps I just didn't like steak.

26

After the disappointing meal, I bought a cold Carlsberg from a nearby shop and walked back to the central part of Old Town where most of the bars were located.

Whilst walking down a side street, I noticed a small bar called Oh My! which had a sign on it saying "Open Mic." I stopped before it and lit a cigarette. I recalled having once written a stand-up routine that had consisted mostly of suicide jokes. Of course, I hadn't dared present it anywhere. However, I still remembered most of it and I could probably ad-lib some things here and there, as long as I disguised them as comedy. So why not give it a try? It was something I wouldn't have normally dared to do, but at the moment it didn't seem as though I had anything to lose.

I finished my cigarette and beer, threw the bottle away, and walked in the door. The bar was small on the inside with low ceilings, a dark décor, red curtains, a small stage, and various old-fashioned posters adorning the walls. I guess you might say it had the atmosphere of a speakeasy. About a quarter of the seats were filled and there was a young woman on stage.

I went to the bar counter and ordered a beer and

whiskey. "What do I have to do to perform?" I asked the bartender as he was pouring me my drinks.

"You want to perform on the Open Mic?"

"Yes."

"Okay, not a problem. We just started. In addition to her," he pointed to the woman on stage," two more people have currently signed up. You can go after them. You've got fifteen minutes. What's your name?"

I gave him my name and he wrote it down on a piece of paper. Then I took my beer and whiskey and found a place to sit a little further from the stage. I left the whiskey for later and sipped on my beer whilst listening to the person on stage. She seemed to be talking about a bunch of female-specific things which I couldn't have given less of a fuck about.

The next guy was no better. His idiotic jokes about Estonians, Russians, toilets, and farting might have entertained the audience, but they did nothing for me. I poured the remaining beer down my throat and went to buy a new one. During the two acts, more people had gathered in the bar. The small venue was almost full by now, and I was beginning to get nervous about going on stage. At least there was going to be another mediocre comedian in the spotlight before me, I thought, which gave me the chance to become a little more drunk before going up on stage.

The third performer was a sweaty and nerdy young man with a trembling voice. He told jokes about cats, dogs, video games and god only knows what else, which was all about as funny as dying of cancer.

My name was called after him. Suddenly, going on stage to perform in front of a bunch of strangers no longer seemed like such a good idea, but it was too late to back down. Given what they had laughed at, it was very likely that my sense of humor wouldn't appeal to this audience—and probably to most audiences—but what the hell. If they wanted to hate me, so be it. I wasn't going to hold back.

I poured the whiskey down my throat, stood up and walked on stage. "Hi there," I said, squinting in front of the bright lights. "I would like to start with a list of things I want to do before I die. Item number one—kill myself." I was silent for a moment. "That's it. It's a short list."

The audience's reaction was deader than a grave.

"Okay. Let me ask you something. Have you ever accidentally dropped your keys in front of your apartment door and thought, oh great, I might as well just kill myself? Or is that too dramatic of a reaction?"

Again, no one laughed.

"Right. My therapist told me to try everything at least once. So I tried committing suicide." I put my fingers to one side of my head and imitated a gun blowing out my brains.

"That's not funny!" someone in the audience said.

"Yeah," someone agreed with him. "What the hell's wrong with you?"

"Humor is subjective," I said. "For example, I

found the last performer to be about as funny as molesting children." I sensed the anger growing in the room. "But I digress. I guess suicide jokes are an acquired taste. Much like being attracted to children. So let's try something else."

I thought for a moment before continuing. "I recently saw a video online of ISIS burning two captured Turkish soldiers alive." I shook my head dramatically. "Let me tell you. Best orgasm I ever had."

One person chuckled.

"All right. Moving on to a more complex topic. We all have moms and dads, right? Or, well, *had* if you're an orphan. But in any case, we all have or have had parents. Including Adolf Hitler. Now some people like to ask, 'If you had the opportunity to travel back in time, would you kill Hitler as a child?' And most people say that they would indeed. Especially the Jews, although they might want to torture him a bit first.

"But let's say you kill him—push him down the stairs, hit him in the head with a hammer, put a bullet in his brain, whatever. So what's then stopping his parents from having another child? And what prevents this new child from being even worse than Hitler? Let's say you kill Hitler and then you come back to the present and the people who sent you back tell you, 'I'm afraid we'll have to send you back again. This time to kill yourself before you kill Hitler, because it turns out that Hitler number two is ten times worse. I guess we should have been more grateful with the Hitler we already had.'

"So what do you do? The answer is simple. Instead of killing Hitler, you kill his worthless fucking parents instead who are responsible for his birth and therefore also for World War II and the Holocaust. Because you see, even serial killers have parents. And had the parents not given birth to them, there wouldn't have been a serial killer. So who's *really* responsible for their murders?

"Because why should we gamble with people's lives? Yes, your child may be the next Albert Einstein. But he may also be the next Albert Fish, who killed, raped, and ate children. And even if they're not going to become Adolf Hitler or serial killers—or their victims—there's still a hell of a big chance that they're going to be just like their mommy and daddy—in other words, worthless." A part of the audience started booing me. I put the microphone closer to my mouth and added, "Just like this audience."

At this, someone hurled a bottle towards me, which hit me square in the face. "Motherfuck—" I put my hand against my face which began pulsating with pain.

The bartender came on stage. "Time to leave," he said.

"Why? I didn't throw the fucking bottle!"

"All the same." He grabbed me by the arm and forced me off the stage.

"You see?" I yelled at the audience as the bartender was escorting me out of the bar. "You're all fucking worthless! You only wanna hear what you already believe. You should have all been aborted!"

When we got out of the bar, the bartender pushed me on the ground. "Dude, you need to seek help. Seriously." He turned around and walked back to the bar.

"And where, pray tell, would I find it?" I yelled after him. I got up from the ground and looked around. Two passers-by stared at me across the road. "What?" I motioned to them with my face, and they moved on.

I sat down on the steps of a nearby building and lit a cigarette. There was a little blood trickling from my eyebrow; I located a crumpled napkin in my pocket and put it against the wound. I heard laughter from inside the bar. They were either making fun of me or they had already forgotten me and moved on. The freak had left the stage and relatable normalcy had returned.

I blew out a large cloud of cigarette smoke and watched it rise towards the dark sky. Suddenly, I felt very lonely. "I'm a lone wolf," I silently quoted from an old movie to an invisible audience, "barking in a corner, plain disgusted with a world I never made and don't want none of."

I stood up and flicked my cigarette against the bar window, sparks flying off it.

27

I WAS WALKING AROUND Old Town, smoking cigarettes, trying to find a bar where to settle down. Somewhere where it was quiet and dark, with few people.

I kept thinking about what the people in the stand-up place thought of me. Probably that I was mentally ill. Hell, I had thought that myself once. I had even tried antidepressants. But their effect was minimal, and when I suddenly stopped taking them, I felt lower than ever. Besides, antidepressants were just another drug. Like alcohol. The difference was, I preferred alcohol.

I had also tried therapy a few times. The last time I did, it went something like this:

"So what brings you here?"

"Pressure from parents. There's nothing really wrong with me other than seeing things too clearly."

"And what is it that you see too clearly?"

"The illusions surrounding us."

"Would you care to elaborate on that?"

"Sure. Most people are indoctrinated by what their parents tell them, what they are told in school, in the workplace, by the government and the media. They think that they should get married, have children, have a career, be patriotic, and so on. But why? Where do these presumptions come from? From nowhere. People have merely been doing all this for a long time, and each generation keeps blindly imitating the previous one, thinking that what they are doing is all terribly meaningful. When in truth it's not. In fact, there is *nothing* meaningful in this world. The world is just a meaningless chaos. Yet they want you to believe that life in this world makes sense, that people in high positions know what they are doing, that the world has direction. But it's all bullshit. And almost no one seems to realize this."

"Oh, you're far from the only person to think that way. We've all been young once."

"Of course. That old excuse. Everyone has their doubts about the world when they're young, but as they get older, they stop rebelling against society and embrace its rules. But this isn't true. What really happens is that people just give up. Because they get tired of fighting against the world's absurdity. Because it's easier that way. You get along with others. You're more successful, happier, more satisfied. At least as long as you can believe in your own bullshit. But once you've given up, that's it. The next thing you know, you have a career, you're married, you have kids, a house, a mortgage, a car, you have acquaintances over for weekend dinners, all that shit. In other words, you're dead."

"But what's wrong with all that? These things give life meaning."

"They do. If you can believe in all that. But it's not real. It's theater. It's a bunch of actors performing a pre-written play called 'How to Behave Like a Human Being.'"

"What you're saying sounds very nihilistic."

"No shit."

"But belief in things is important. Without it, there's no reason to do anything."

"Exactly. There isn't. And there's no basis for believing in anything either, especially that a particular pattern of behavior is sane and if you don't behave that way—if you don't want a family or a house or children for example or even to exist at all—well, then you must be crazy. Because in this world you are only accepted as long as you believe in its illusions. And that's what your profession is all about. You are the protectors of society's illusions."

"I'm sorry you feel that way."

But he wasn't sorry. Not at all. In fact, he was probably glad to have gotten rid of me. Because in order for therapy to "work," it was necessary to believe in it. Which was something I wasn't capable of. Mental illness, as Thomas Szasz had revealed, was only a myth that was used to control people. Just like religion. The secular man ultimately went to the psychologist for the same reason that the religious man went to the priest. As for me, I preferred to go to the bottle instead.

I stopped walking. I had found the place I had been looking for.

28

THE NAME OF THE bar was Calavera, and it had a large sugar skull on its sign. The bar was underground and shadowy, just as I preferred.

I walked up to the counter and ordered a beer. As the bartender was pouring it, I noticed a digital juke-box on one of the walls. I dug a fifty-cent coin out of my pocket and inserted it into the opening. The song I chose was "The End" by The Doors. Whilst paying for the beer, I asked the bartender whether he could turn the volume up on the music. He said he would.

I then found a seat in the darkest corner of the bar and sat down. Holding a napkin over my busted eye-brow and sipping on the beer, I looked around. The bar had a Mexican Day of the Dead theme with lots of paper skeletons and sugar skulls and colorful perforated paper banners hanging over the ceiling. Although celebrating Day of the Dead may have sounded morbid, I knew that what the Mexicans actually believed in was that after their deaths their souls migrated to the Land of the Dead and on Day of the Dead merely came back to visit them.

For some reason, it was damned hard for most people to accept the most obvious fact in the entire universe—that when you were dead, you were dead, that's it. Nothing came after death. The person you were ceased to be. Because the person you were was just the result of your brain activity. Your consciousness and your personality were neurochemical illusions. And when the brain stopped working, you ceased to be. Science had proven long ago that there were no souls or an afterlife. Yet this did not stop people from claiming that no one knew what came after death, whilst the truth was that *everyone* knew. Most just didn't have the courage to admit it.

I was just about finished with my beer when I noticed that a big husky guy sitting next to a horse-faced woman—presumably his girlfriend—was staring at me. He seemed quite drunk. Why he was staring at me, I didn't know, but I stared right back, motioning, "What?" with my face. Perhaps he hadn't agreed with my somber choice of music. Or perhaps he just didn't like my face, which wouldn't have been the first time.

I soon needed a new beer, so I went to the bar counter and waited for the bartender to show up; he had seemingly disappeared somewhere in the back room. I was the only person in the line.

The big guy who had been staring at me suddenly stepped behind me. "Move," he said.

I turned around and looked at him. "Excuse me?"

"I said move."

I looked to my left and to my right and spread my hands in confusion. "But I'm the only person in the line."

"Move out of the way," he said impatiently.

"But I was here before you."

"You wanna fucking go outside?"

"What for? A date? Are you sure your girlfriend won't mind?"

His face turned red. "You trying to pick a fight with me? Want me to knock your fucking teeth out?"

"You confused yourself with me, didn't you?"

"What?"

I spoke more slowly so he could understand me. "I meant that *you* were the one picking a fight, not me. But whatever. I'd be delighted to come outside with you. Let's go."

"All right," he growled, and started walking towards the exit.

I walked after him and inconspicuously grabbed a can of pepper spray from my coat pocket, which I palmed in my hand like a magician. I wasn't stupid. This guy weighed at least twice as much as I did. He could probably knock me out with a single punch.

We climbed the stairs that led to the front of the bar. The street outside was empty. We stood in the middle of the narrow cobblestone street as if we were characters in the video game *Street Fighter*.

My opponent appeared to be semicomatose, probably on account of the large amounts of alcohol he had consumed. "Well?" I said, which seemed to have woken him up.

He took a step towards me and lifted his hand. Before he could strike, however, I stretched out my hand and began pepper spraying him in the face, which he didn't even seem to register at first. He took another step towards me, whilst I took a step back, still holding down the button on the pepper spray can; when the can was about two thirds empty, he finally stopped moving. He suddenly put his hands against his eyes, as if he had just realized what had happened, and began howling in pain.

His horse-faced girlfriend came out of the bar and started yelling at me. "What do you think you're doing?!" she shrieked, going to the guy's aid.

"What am *I* doing? I'm teaching him a lesson, that's all. *He's* the one who attacked me."

She looked sternly at the can of pepper spray in my hand. "And that gives you the right to pepper spray him in the face?"

"Why yes. It does, in fact."

"But he's a boxer! And he's drunk!" She helped the boxer, who was now crying like a little girl, sit down on the sidewalk.

"Lady, in what universe is *that* an excuse?" I searched for a cigarette. "Listen, if you don't want this happening again in the future, I'd advise keeping this Mongoloid on a leash."

I lit the cigarette and began walking away. I'd had enough of Old Town.

29

I WAS WALKING THROUGH the pedestrian tunnel at the Kaubamaja intersection when I was suddenly stopped by a man in a gray raincoat who had some books under his arm. He asked me whether he could talk to me for a bit.

"All right," I said, giving him the benefit of the doubt. "What do you want to talk about?"

"About God." He had a slight Russian accent.

I sighed. "Then I'm afraid you have the wrong person."

"You don't believe in God?"

"It's not that I don't believe in God; it's that there is no God."

"Is that so? And then how do you explain how we got here?"

"Through evolution." He chuckled mockingly at my answer, as if I had said something *really* stupid. "It's a well-established fact," I added.

"Okay. If you believe in evolution so much, tell me just one thing. Where are all the fossils?"

"Are you serious?"

"Yes."

"There are thousands of fossils."

"Name me one."

"Name you one?"

"Yes."

Oh great. Another fucking Mongoloid.

"Well," I began, "there's a recent one found in Africa called *Australopithecus*, from which Homo sapiens evolved. It's essentially halfway between a monkey and a human. And they found an almost complete skeleton. So in fact there *are* fossils. And this is just one of many."

He waved his hand dismissively. "Ah, that's just a monkey."

"It's not 'just a monkey.' It's a being that is an intermediate between a monkey and a human. Although even that is an oversimplification since evolution has many branches and a monkey can evolve into various different beings. The fact that man evolved from a monkey is just an old and idiotic misunderstanding. In truth there are various primate genera, only one of which led to a human being."

"Listen, I *know* things. I have a university degree.

"In what field?"

"I'm an electrical engineer."

"And what does that have to do with evolution?"

"I'm just saying I know how things work."

"Maybe about electricity, but you clearly don't know anything about evolution. Maybe you should read a few books on it?"

"Or maybe *you* should read some of the books *I*

have here?" He raised his eyebrows, showing me the books under his arm; it was a bunch of religious shit with bad cover art.

"No thanks. I'm too old for fairy tales."

"Ah, but maybe your evolution is a fairy tale?"

"Unfortunately for you, there is a lot of evidence for evolution, whereas there is not a single shred of evidence for your beliefs."

"You don't know what you're talking about, my friend."

"No, it is you who doesn't know what he's talking about. God does not exist, has never existed, and will never exist. We're all alone in this universe. All alone. And that's a fact."

He began to get emotional. "I know in my heart that God exists. And I don't need any evidence for that."

I let out a deep sigh. "All right. Let's say he exists. Let's say God exists and he created this world. But have you looked at the world around you?" I pointed all around me. "It's a nightmare. War, rape, torture, murder, disease, corruption, insanity. If God created all these things, he must be a psychopath. Or, as you like to say, if he gave humans free will—which is scientifically impossible—and then watched on as we tortured and killed each other in record numbers, he obviously doesn't give a shit about us. So if God exists—which he doesn't—he not only doesn't love you, but in all likelihood he fucking hates you! Now, if you don't mind,

I'm gonna go and get drunk. So long."

I started walking away.

"You're gonna burn in hell, my friend!" he called out to me.

"We're already in hell," I said and continued walking.

30

I HAD AT FIRST thought of going to some bar outside of Old Town, but then I changed my mind. What I really needed was to get away from bars. If only for a while. But I didn't want to go home, and there were no friends to visit.

I could thus think of only one place left to go. My old home. Where my mother and half-sister lived. And my stepfather, even though he could hardly be called that since all the time I had known him, he had only shown complete indifference towards me. Much like my father.

My relationship with my mother and sister wasn't much better. In fact, there was no relationship as such; there was only utter disinterest. I might as well have grown up an orphan. It was clear that they had all been glad when I finally left home in order to be miserable elsewhere.

The bus stop from which the bus went to the suburbs where they lived was nearby. I walked there and inspected the timetable; the next bus left in ten minutes. I lit a Marlboro Red.

After I had waited for a few minutes, I was approached by a middle-aged man with curly hair and a mustache who sort of looked like Kurt Vonnegut.

"I'll be honest with you," he said. "I'm not gonna ask you for money. I'll just point out the drugs that I need in the pharmacy."

"I'm sorry, what?"

"Got the shakes, you see." He showed me his hands, which were slightly trembling. "Get dizzy spells now and then. Need medicine for that."

"Okay. But why are you asking *me*?"

"Got no money."

"Can't you get government help for that?"

"Bah!" He waved his hand dismissively. "The government don't help."

"Are you sure about that?"

"Wait." He put his hand on my shoulder and staggered a bit. "Getting one of them dizzy spells again."

I took a step back. "Well, I'm sorry, but I can't help you. You must have expected that asking random strangers on the street to buy you medicine isn't gonna go so well."

His expression suddenly turned sour. "So much for loving your neighbor!" He spat on the ground. "In truth it's every man for his fuckin' self, ain't it?"

"That's right. Because you're not my neighbor. No one is. We're all strangers, you see. And we all have our problems. Including me."

"Yeah . . ." His voice trailed off, a disgusted look on his face.

After that, the bus arrived, and I got on. I watched

from the bus window, as the man kept staring into the void. Maybe his illness had been an act. Or maybe not. But let's say it wasn't. So what? There were millions of people suffering and dying at any given moment on this wonderful little globe of ours. More than twenty thousand people alone died of hunger each day, half of them children, their only crime having been born into this monstrous world.

Of course, you didn't have to be hungry to suffer. If my parents had known in advance how unhappy I would become, how I would end up despising the world, would they still have decided to have me? Would they have been so cruel? In fact, wasn't I ultimately even more miserable than the wretch I had just spoken to? At least *his* suffering was physical and could be treated by medicine, whereas mine was a side effect of having understood the malignant uselessness of existence. So why did he deserve more help than the millions of other sufferers, myself included? And how the hell was I supposed to help someone else when I couldn't even help myself?

The bus arrived at my destination, and I stepped off. It was dark outside, and the air was crisp. It was about a ten-minute walk to my parents' house. For some reason, I still had the habit of calling them my parents, even though, just like my father, they barely were, one less than the other.

I lit a cigarette and started walking along the path towards their house. The walk brought forth memories of various other times that I had walked the same path, some of them good, some of them bad, most of them forgotten. To my left and right sat many identical houses in which lived identical families with identical thoughts. I noticed that unlike the last time I had visited them, even more of the forest had been cut down in the area to build even more identical houses where new identical families with identical thoughts would soon move in.

When I got to my parents' house, I rang the doorbell and waited. No one answered. I rang again. Nothing.

Fuck. They were probably out socializing. The trip had been for nothing. I let out a long sigh. Well, since I still had the key, I might as well enter. Perhaps there'd be some beer in the fridge.

The inside of the house looked like it always had. Normal. I walked over to the fridge and grabbed a beer. Then I walked to my old room and opened the door. The room had a black wooden floor, dark green walls, and a chrome ceiling fan. A black desk and office chair used to be placed in it as if it were a detective office.

Well, I *had* been a detective of sorts. An existential detective that had been searching for the meaning of life. However, in the end all the leads turned out to be false and I hadn't been able to find any.

The room was undoubtedly the most beautiful in the house and it was now being used for storage as well as to accommodate guests. As I walked around the room, I remembered the hundreds of film noirs I had watched in it. The magic tricks I had practiced for hours on end. The philosophers I had read. The pornography I had consumed. The girlfriends I had fucked. The alcohol I had drank. The drama. The isolation. The depression. My hopes and fears. And my tears.

I walked over to the bookshelf; on it stood some books I had left behind, among them Emil Cioran's *The Trouble with Being Born.*

I opened it on one of my favorite passages and read:

The same feeling of not belonging, of futility, wherever I go: I pretend interest in what matters nothing to me, I bestir myself mechanically or out of charity, without ever being caught up, without ever being somewhere. What attracts me is elsewhere, and I don't know where that elsewhere is.

I had left this book of philosophical pessimism behind as a kind of morbid joke, hoping that my mother would one day discover it. This of course wasn't very likely because, as little as I had seen her read, it tended to be the same pile of lies that most people read since it fed into their illusions—self-help books.

I had always found it funny how the authors of self-help books became rich and famous solely through selling their self-help books, and how no one had even heard of them before. That's because they were usually random people with no qualifications whatsoever who one day just suddenly appeared from somewhere, promising to solve all of your problems and make you rich and successful with just one lousy book. It was an offer that the average person found hard to refuse. Indeed, some of them had dozens of such books on their bookshelf. Yet unsurprisingly, they didn't seem to be of any help. The only person they helped, in fact, was the author. Financially. Bad taste, as Bukowski said, created far more millionaires than good taste. And to understand how truly bad the average person's taste was, it was enough to consider what the most popular book of all time was—the Bible.

As I was standing in my old room, I suddenly heard someone push a key in the keyhole of the front door. I put the book away and went to see who it was—it was my half-sister.

"Brother!" she said. "What are you doing here?"

It was true that I had rarely visited them since I had moved out. But I was like a vampire; I only visited when I was invited. Which was rare. Perhaps it was because I tended to suck the joy out of every place I went to.

"I was just in the neighborhood and thought I'd drop by," I lied. "Where's everyone else? I saw both cars parked in front of the house."

"Both mom and dad are at a birthday. They took a taxi and said they wouldn't be home until midnight.

Are you going to wait for them?"

"Nah. I'll just come back another day."

"Oh, okay."

I took a sip of beer. "So where are you coming from?"

"From a friend's house."

"Uh-huh. And how's school?" I couldn't think of anything else to ask.

"What do you think?"

"It . . . sucks?"

"Exactly."

"Thought so."

I picked up my phone and ordered a taxi. "I'll be on my way then."

"Okay. Do you want me to tell mom and dad you were here?"

I poured the last drop of beer down my throat. "Only in case they ask who drank the beer." I put on my coat. "I'll be going then. Be good."

"Bye."

Outside, I lit a cigarette and looked towards the night sky. When I had lived there, I had often gazed at the stars, which were well visible due to the low amount of light pollution. I had even seen the northern lights there once. At the moment, however, the sky was overcast, and nothing could be seen.

After I got in the taxi, I told the driver to take me downtown. Back to the bars. Back to booze. Back to misery. Back to ruin. My natural habitat.

31

ONCE IN TOWN, I decided to give Scarlet Emperor another shot. It was almost midnight.

I stepped inside and ordered a beer. It was much more lively in there than it had been the last time. When the bartender finished pouring my beer, I went to the smoking room. There were several people inside. One of them was standing alone by the window, smoking a cigarette. She looked like a college student.

I walked over to her and lit a cigarette. "Good evening," I said.

She looked towards me briefly and said, "Hello."

I remained silent afterwards to see if she was interested in having a conversation with me. After a few minutes, she turned her head towards me and asked the most common of all questions—what did I do?

"I think and I drink."

"Do you study?"

"I'm an academician of no academy. What about you? Do you study?"

"I do."

"What do you study?"

"Physics."

"Hmm. Interesting." I flicked my cigarette into the

metal bucket that was being used as a trash can and asked her whether she would like a drink. She agreed to it. We left the smoking room and sat behind the bar counter.

"So what's your poison?" I asked her. I never asked for people's names. For what was in a name? It was the personality that mattered.

"I'll have a rum and coke."

"Two Cuba Libres, please," I told the bartender.

After the bartender had finished pouring our drinks, the girl asked me, "So what brings you here?"

"Superdeterminism," I replied.

"What?"

"I assume you're familiar with quantum mechanics?"

She sucked her drink through a straw. "I am."

I removed the straw from my drink and took a sip. "In that case, you're probably aware of the different interpretations of quantum mechanics, such as the Copenhagen interpretation, Bohm's interpretation, the many-worlds interpretation and so on."

"I've heard of them, yes."

"However, I bet you haven't heard of the only interpretation which happens to be true."

"Which is?"

"Superdeterminism."

"And why do you think it's true?"

"Because it's the only interpretation that doesn't presuppose the existence of free will."

"Don't tell me you don't believe in free will?"

"Well, as we know, classical physics tells us that for every action there is an equal and opposite reaction."

"Newton's Third Law."

"Yes. And thus, since objects only react with each other mechanically, there remains no place for free will."

"Well, yeah, but quantum mechanics is different because it uses probabilities, and so free will *is* possible."

"Yes. As long as you believe in interpretations that allow it. But if you *really* think about it, free will is not even possible as a concept because everything in the universe can either be predetermined or random. And in either case there is no free will. Of course, the universe is both random and predetermined at the same time, because the Big Bang, which set the deterministic trajectory of time, was, as far as we know, a random event. And yet, everything *after* it has since been one hundred percent deterministic, with no atom being anywhere it wasn't supposed to be."

I took a sip from my drink. My companion didn't seem terribly interested, but she was still listening.

"Superdeterminism," I continued, "argues that since there has been no freedom of choice since the beginning of the universe, every scientific measurement has been predetermined. And as you probably know, interpretations of quantum mechanics are mostly based on the two-slit experiment and assume that the result of the experiment depends on whether it is measured by a conscious observer or not. However, if there is no free will, the so-called choice to measure it was predetermined, and so was the result, which means that the result does not depend on the conscious observer. This means that there is no measurement problem in quantum mechanics and therefore probabilities do not exist. And that, in turn, means that quantum mechanics is just as deterministic as classical physics, and that every last thing that has ever happened was destined to happen from the very beginning of the universe."

"Okay, but why do most scientists then say that quantum mechanics allows free will?"

"Probably because they like the idea that they have free will. As do most people. Or maybe it's because they have no choice."

"And you have?"

"No, I also have no choice about what I say. Just as I have no choice as to whether or not I'm sitting here right now."

"You *really* believe that?"

"Well, of course it *seems* to me that I have free will, as it seems to you and everyone else. But this is just an illusion, just like when we watch the sun rise in the morning, when in fact it is the Earth rotating on its axis towards the sun. Research has shown that the conscious idea that we *could* have done something different comes about a second after the brain has already made the decision."

"I think the question here is more how to interpret the results of the study."

"No, the question is, why did the universe create the illusion of free will? And the answer is that it created it for the same reason that it created all illusions, such as happiness and love—because it was destined to create them. Why was it destined to create them? Because our universe is just one of an infinite number of other universes with random properties that arose randomly through quantum fluctuations. One random feature of our universe, for instance, is life. There may not be life in most universes. There may not even be planets or light. Some, on the other hand, may have no light, whilst having planets and beings. In some universes there may be beings more advanced than us who are not even conscious. And some universes themselves may be conscious—but only for a limited amount of time due to entropy. And yes, I know what you're thinking right now. That this is just my opinion and nothing else."

"You're right. That's exactly what I'm thinking."

"And you're right, of course. It *is* just my opinion. However, if we accept that no one has had any freedom of choice since the beginning of the universe, which is what superdeterminism presupposes, this means that me sitting here and talking with you right now has been predestined since the beginning of the universe. As was pedophilia, cannibalism, rape, and murder. Not to mention the plagues and wars and serial killers. In fact, if we add up all the horrors that have ever been committed on this planet, then God, if we were to call the universe that—as did Einstein and Spinoza—is a malevolent scumbag, a cosmic torturer, and the king of psychopaths. But since God doesn't really have free will either, it is perhaps more fitting to say that the Big Bang was God committing suicide, and we are merely the maggots devouring his rotting carcass, which eventually will vanish due to cosmic decay, aka entropy. And thank God for that!"

She was staring at me with a bewildered expression. It took a while before she managed to open her mouth. "Do you know what I think?" she asked.

"What?"

"I think it's time for me to leave." She got up from her seat and walked away, leaving her drink unfinished.

"Where are you going?" I cried out to her, louder than I had intended. Here I was revealing to her the secrets of the universe, only to be treated like a leper for doing so.

"Calm down," the bartender told me. "Otherwise, you'll have to leave."

"Oh what a tragedy that would be," I said sarcastically. I gulped down my drink and the girl's, and then ordered a beer and a shot of whiskey. The bartender poured me my drinks, disgust reflecting off his face.

I was beginning to get a bad case of the fuck-its. I downed the whiskey and used the beer as a chaser. I then ordered a shot of Jägermeister and downed that. Then a shot of Sambuca. Then vodka. Then tequila. And, finally, a shot of absinthe.

After I was done with all the shots, each adding fuel to my fire, I was beginning to feel like some sort of philosophical Tony Montana. I got up from my seat, the world spinning around me.

"You know what?" I said out loud towards no one in particular. "None of you people know fuckin' anything!" A few people turned around and looked towards me. "About life. About the world. About the secret truths of the universe. You don't know shit! You live your whole lives in delirium, and you die as stupid as you lived. And when someone is trying to tell you something *real* for a change, someone who has put their very sanity on the line in order to learn of these things, you spit in their fuckin' face!" I gestured aggressively with my hands. "Why? Because it threatens the nice little fantasy world you've built for yourself, where everything is good and beautiful and meaningful all the time and where you're able to achieve anything you set your mind to. Unfortunately, there's just one little problem with your fantasy, folks. IT'S FUCKING BULLSHIT!"

After that, someone—either the bartender or a security guard, I couldn't see exactly—grabbed me from behind and put me in a stranglehold. He began forcing me out of the bar, while the people in the bar looked on and commented.

"Take your . . . fucking hands . . . off me!" I said gutturally, half suffocating.

He forced me through the bar door and pushed me towards the stairs that led to the exit on the first floor. When we reached the first step, however, I suddenly lost my balance, after which the guy holding me let go of me and I tumbled down the stairs.

And then there was only darkness.

32

I WAS TRAPPED IN a giant spiderweb that lay suspended in nothingness. I looked up. Above me hung a gigantic black spider, its fangs glistening. It began pulling me towards her.

I opened my eyes. A little bit of sunlight was filtering in through the window blinds to my right. The walls of the room were white, and the floor was covered in linoleum. A smell of antiseptic hung in the air. I realized I was in a hospital bed. It was one of the last places I wanted to be.

I had already seen plenty of hospitals in my life. I had been a sickly child. I'd had my appendix, adenoids, and tonsils removed. I'd had a broken arm. And, like Bukowski, I'd had terrible acne. All of this had led to plenty of time spent in hospitals, allowing me to see their clinical ugliness up close. The old, nearly dead people shuffling through its corridors, barely knowing who they were anymore. The morbidly obese mountains of fat barely fitting in hospital beds. The lifelong smokers coughing up bits of their lungs. The stroke victims. The genetic defects. The suicide attempts. The weakness and decay. The endless ailments, both physical and imaginary. The doctors like priests. The nurses like nuns. And the patients like feeble-minded church-goers, seeking salvation for the sickness in their souls—the sickness of life—a sickness that only death could cure. If the human body was so fragile that it constantly needed medical care, it couldn't be worth very much.

I sighed. Right. But what had brought me there? There were numerous bruises on my body. I touched my head; there was a big band aid on it. I figured I must have banged my head when I had fallen down the stairs in Scarlet Emperor, right before I lost consciousness.

I looked around the room. In addition to me, there was an old man lying on a bed across the room from me, reading a newspaper. My clothes were placed on a chair next to the bed. A nurse must have undressed me.

It didn't take long for me to decide that I was going to leave, and that no one was going to stop me. I silently got up and got dressed. After going to the toilet and removing the band aid from my head, I walked to the door of the room.

"Where are you going?" the old man suddenly asked in a weak voice, putting down his newspaper.

"I'm leaving."

"Why?"

"Because I don't need to be here."

"I think you'd better wait for the nurse."

"I'm afraid she cannot help me, old man."

As I pressed down on the door handle, the old man

suddenly yelled, to the best of his ability, "Nurse!"

I left the room quickly. In the hallway, I headed for the stairwell, trying to avoid eye contact with the nurses. No one stopped me as I slipped into the staircase.

It was only when I arrived outside that I recognized the hospital. I had visited its emergency department once because of severe abdominal pains. At the time, it had felt like I was dying, but when I got to the hospital the pain had suddenly disappeared. Ever since then, however, I'd been afraid of stomach aches. Which meant that suicide through pills was ruled out for me.

I dug out a cigarette and lit it. I checked my pockets. My wallet, phone, apartment keys, the half-empty can of pepper spray, and flask were all there. There was even a little whiskey left inside the flask. I uncorked it and took a hit; it tasted damn good.

I looked at the time on my phone; it was five in the evening. I didn't want to go back to my apartment yet. For I knew what awaited me there. And so, the only logical conclusion that remained was to go to a bar.

Yeah, I was a broken record all right.

33

THE HOSPITAL WAS IN the Russian part of town. It was an industrial district with no industry, full of Soviet-era brutalist architecture. Its inhabitants lived in massive gray concrete apartment blocks with hundreds of small and identical apartments. The atmosphere of the oppressive regime that built them still lingered in the air, even though it was now nothing but a cheap and ugly district full of urban decay. As were its inhabitants.

I walked between the gray concrete buildings for a while, smoking cigarettes. The sky was beginning to turn dark. It was going to rain.

Considering my surroundings, I decided to go to a bar I wouldn't have normally visited. A Russian bar. Based on my experience, it was probable that I'd get beaten up in one. But I didn't care. It would just be one more thing to push me over the edge. And given that I was afraid of heights, I'd welcome the push. Because the carousel of life was wearing very thin at this point, and I didn't much feel like going for another ride. When an amusement park stopped being amusing, it was time to leave. And that's exactly what this world was in the end. Just a pointless waste of time. A bunch of colorful flashing lights and superficial attractions that mechanically kept repeating and repeating until you finally got sick of it all.

I eventually found a suitably suspicious-looking bar in a dilapidated old brick building with a generic green neon sign that said Bar & Billiards. Two mean-looking Russians were smoking cigarettes at its entrance, eyeing me as I stepped past them. It was as though they could smell that I wasn't a Russian.

I sat on a worn bar stool in front of the worn-out counter. Everything in the bar had a sort of worn look to it, as though it was from the nineties. And regardless of the sign outside, I didn't see any billiards tables anywhere.

"One Carlsberg please," I told the bartender with a worn-out look on her face when she finally paid attention to me. She didn't appear to speak any Estonian or English, so I pointed to the bottle and used sign language. This she understood.

After the horror of waking up in the hospital, the cold beer tasted extremely good. There were few pleasures in life that were comparable to the first beer of the day. I practically inhaled it down and ordered another one.

As I had expected, I soon caught the eye of a Russian who, for one reason or another, just didn't seem to like the fact that I existed. Well, that's how it was with some of these Russians in Estonia. It was sometimes enough to just glance towards a mean-looking one and they already thought you were looking for trouble. I figured it was because the majority population resented the poverty of the minority population, which, among other things, bred crime. And the minority population, in turn, resented the majority population for not doing enough to help with their poor living conditions. The situation was perhaps comparable to the hostility between black and white people in America.

Every country had its ghettos, as they say. And in Estonia these were the Russian parts of town, such as the one I was in. What made it particularly hilarious was that, aside from a few curse words, I didn't speak a word of Russian. And if you didn't speak any Russian, the Russians looked down on you, even though they were a minority in your own country. Of course, they themselves thought nothing of not knowing any Estonian, even if they had lived there their whole lives.

After having stared at me for a while, the Russian finally walked over and started picking a fight with me. He said something in Russian and chuckled.

"I'm sorry," I said, "but I don't speak Russian."

He repeated what he said before.

"I told you I don't speak Russian."

He pushed me in the shoulder.

"The hell's your problem?"

He pushed me again.

"Right. I guess I'll fuck off then." I poured the beer down my throat, got up, and started walking out of the bar.

It was raining outside. I stood under the cover in front of the bar and tried lighting a cigarette when the same Russian suddenly grabbed me by the shoulder and started pushing me into the alley next to the bar. "Ah, here we go again," I said, not putting up any resistance. "First the boxer and now this guy."

We stopped near some dumpsters. "Što takoi?" he said, staring into my eyes, his face red with anger.

"You know, you really found the wrong person to pick a fight with. And it's not because I'm a tough guy like you're pretending to be. It's because I don't care whether I live or die. Which means there's nothing you can threaten me with, you Russian cunt."

"Što!?" It was as though he couldn't comprehend the fact that I didn't speak any Russian.

"Listen, if you don't speak any Estonian or even English for Christ's sake, then maybe you should fuck off back to Russia, huh? Why are you even here?"

"Idi nahui suka bljad!" he politely informed me.

"Oh really? Okay. Well, what would you do if I told you the following: why don't you go and suck Putin's cock!"

He punched me in the face. The blow landed on my right eye. My face was numb with pain. I waited until my senses returned before saying, "I thought you didn't speak Estonian."

He took out a small handgun from his jacket pocket and pointed it at me. "You want die?" he said with a thick Russian accent.

Ah, so he apparently did speak some English, even though it was probably just something he'd heard in a Steven Seagal action movie. Of course, it wasn't hard for me to come up with an answer to his question. "Believe it or not, I do."

"Što!?" He shoved the gun in my face, pushing it against my cheek. Although my heart was pounding with adrenaline, the situation did not cause me as much fear as it would have to most people because, unlike them, it wasn't death that I was afraid of; it was life. Besides, I had fantasized about this happening many times, albeit in my fantasy I was the one holding the gun, pointing it at myself.

"Let me help you with that," I said, slowly placing the fingers of my left hand on the gun barrel and gently nudging it towards my forehead. This was also something I had seen in a movie. "There. That's better. Now you can pull the trigger." His eyes seemed bewildered by my action. I could tell from his composure that he wasn't going to go through with it. After all, it wasn't the nineties anymore.

However, the moment was simply too good to let it pass. My planned method of suicide had been to hang myself. But fate, it seemed, had now presented me with a much better option. A bullet in the brain didn't hurt. And it was easy to pull a trigger.

Whilst I was holding the gun against my forehead with my left hand, I had secretly grabbed the can of pepper spray from my coat pocket and palmed it in my right hand—who'd have thought that it would one day be useful to know a few magic tricks.

In one swift motion, I brought my right hand up and shot the pepper spray into his eyes, whilst tightening the grip of my left hand around the gun barrel and yanking it out of his hand. The shock from the pepper spray was enough for him to let go of the gun.

After the can of pepper spray was empty, I pistol whipped him in the face as hard as I could. He fell to his knees and groaned, his hands against his eyes, blood dripping from between his fingers.

After this, my first reaction was to get the fuck away from there as fast as I could. I put the gun in my coat pocket and rushed out of the alley, my heart pumping like a jackhammer. I took various side streets, constantly looking back to make sure that no one was following me. Finally, I found a bus stop and got on the first bus out of there.

I took deep breaths in and out, trying to calm myself down, whilst looking through the rain-streaked window at the large concrete buildings passing by in the distance. The bus was driving through Laagna Channel.

I observed them until I noticed a little kid staring at me in the bus. I realized that the barrel of the gun had been sticking out of my coat pocket. I tucked it inside. The kid was now looking at my face. I lifted my finger to my mouth and made a "shush" motion. He looked away in fright.

When I got off the bus, it was raining heavily. Nevertheless, I decided to walk home. It was a walk to the gallows, but I didn't mind.

34

By the time I got to my apartment complex, I was drenched. I looked inside the mailbox; inside was a letter addressed to me—a rare occurrence. I opened it whilst walking up the stairs.

I stood in front of my apartment door, staring at the letter wide-eyed. It was an eviction notice. I had thirty days to leave the premises. An involuntary smile crept across my face. It seemed God had a sense of humor after all.

I entered the apartment and put the gun on the table. I changed out of my wet clothes and poured myself a drink. I sat on the couch and looked at the gun. I didn't know much about guns, but I had seen this one in enough movies and video games to know that it was a Makarov. I removed the magazine. Inside of it was only one cartridge. But that's all I needed anyway.

I took out the cartridge and studied it between my fingers. How strange that such a small thing could put an end to such a big thing. The thought was tempting. But I decided to postpone it until the next morning. It was best to do mentally taxing things towards the beginning of the day, when the brain was more alert, I reasoned, as it tended to get worn down during the day. And I knew nothing more mentally taxing than the decision to commit suicide, which, as Camus said, was ultimately the only philosophical question that mattered.

I placed the cartridge in the shot glass which I had received from the homeless guy. I then considered what to do with my last night on earth. Drink? Of course. I still had plenty of whiskey left. And alcohol was my oldest friend, after all; in fact, right now it seemed to be my only friend. But beyond that? I thought for a moment. Well, I guess I could put my writing skills to the test for one last time and try writing a decent suicide note. Hadn't I, in a way, already been practicing for it the whole week?

I located a pen and an unused black notebook. I opened the notebook on the first page and wrote "Suicide Note." I decided I was going to write it about whatever came to my mind and that I was going to be completely honest. About everything. Who knows? Maybe it would end up becoming my masterpiece.

I took a sip of whiskey and started writing:

It is said that life flashes before your eyes before you die. This is obviously not true; it's just a Hollywood cliché. But seeing as I have some time to kill before I kill myself, I've decided to briefly write down the predetermined trajectory of my life, which has now brought me to the miserable point where my existence is going to end with an exclamation mark—a bullet from a gun.

So let's start from the very beginning. First came the universe, the beginning of all our troubles. Then came matter, which clustered together to create planets, stars, and so on. On one of these planets a disease developed—a disease called life. It kept evolving into more and more complex forms until one of its forms became man. Inspired mainly by delirium, he eventually took over the land and littered it with his offspring. And from one of these I was born.

I don't remember much from my childhood. Perhaps because there isn't much to remember. But what I do remember is that I grew up in poverty in a one-room apartment. Not that this bothered me at the time of course. For how different everything seems through the naive eyes of a child. How acceptable. How meaningful. Children, as Leopardi said, see everything in nothing, whereas men see nothing in everything.

My parents divorced when I was around seven years old, and I went to live with my mother. Although at the beginning I also occasionally stayed with my father, he eventually moved abroad, and I didn't see him for many years.

My mother and I moved a lot as well, probably because of the poverty. I had moved house more than ten times before I was even a teenager. That may be one of the reasons why I never had any friends.

When I started school, I was an excellent student at

first. This lasted for about four years. Then, for some reason—perhaps because I was slowly beginning to realize the insignificance of everything—my grades suddenly dropped, and my attitude towards school became indifferent. However, I was never punished for this at home. Nor did my parents—for my mom had found another man by then—try to improve my behavior. In fact, no matter what I did, they just seemed to ignore me most of the time, and I was left to my own devices. Both my parents and school were terrible motivators, and I began to see giant cracks in the fictions they spun at an early age, which soon made me no longer have any faith in them at all.

I often felt lonely because I couldn't relate to other schoolmates, despite my best efforts, which were largely pretended. Instead of going out with them—not that they ever invited me—I usually went home after school and watched movies. I watched an average of three movies per day, my only friends being the fictional characters in them. Maybe that's why I couldn't stand most people? How could they possibly compete with the likes of Humphrey Bogart? In any case, movies for me were a refuge from the misery of everyday life. Yet despite my love of movies, I had no realistic ideas what I was going to do with my life. Although I may have wanted to be Kubrick, I wasn't even capable of being Ed Wood.

When I got to high school, I made an effort at first, and in the beginning my grades were good. However, the arbitrary rules of the school system eventually became unbearable to me. Why was I forced to study subjects that were not objectively important or of any interest to me? Why was what was said in each subject presented as if it were an absolute truth that should not be questioned? Why were all the subjects taught in such a dry, boring, and shitty way? Why was skeptical thinking not taught in any of the subjects? Why did the teachers never have proper answers for my questions? Why were they like machines that monotonously repeated the same text they had repeated a thousand times before?

I remember having asked my math teacher "why?" so many times that one day she had a nervous breakdown. She just couldn't explain to me how things worked and why they mattered. It was not customary to question such things. They were supposed to be self-evident. But they weren't.

It was in high school that I became interested in philosophy. The point of philosophy, after all, was to question things that others took for granted. And questioning things seemed to be about the only thing that I was good at, which may have had something to do with the lack of a father figure in my youth. As did my disregard for authority.

Philosophy led me to science and science led me to techno-utopianism. The latter was promoted, for instance, by Jacque Fresco and Ray Kurzweil, whose ideas initially fascinated me. Unfortunately, such ideas had an unpleasant side effect—when you spent a lot of time in your mind in a so-called ideal society, where everything was free and technology did all the unpleasant work for you, our real world began to feel more and more like a miserable prison where we had to slave our lives away without ever having anything to show for it.

Yet I soon realized that such techno-utopian visions of the future were not even close to coming true, because it was clear that our actual world, where eighty-five percent of people are still religious and countries are still at war with one another, is not ready for such advanced thinking. Our actual world, as one Italian anarchist put it, is more of a pestilent church, covetous and slimy, where all have an idol to fetishistically adore and an altar on which to sacrifice themselves.

Disappointed with ideology, I went back to philosophy. It was around this time that I discovered a book by the Romanian philosopher Emil Cioran called *On the Heights of Despair*. It shook my world. Although it was negative to the extreme, it seemed to say exactly what all of my previous knowledge had been hinting at, and which I had suspected for some time now—that we live in a world of delusions in which life consists mostly of pointless suffering and that it would have been better never to have been.

And that is how I discovered the ultimate illusion buster that is philosophical pessimism. Digging deeper into it, I found some rather unique thinkers, such as

Ulrich Horstmann, who found our existence so hopeless that he suggested blowing up the planet with nuclear weapons.

Or Philipp Mainländer, who thought that before the beginning of the universe, there was God. However, *he* concluded that the reason the universe arose was because God wanted to commit suicide. But because God existed outside of time and space, he had to first transform himself into time and space—that is, a universe, which would slowly perish through entropy and eventually become nothing.

The reason God wanted to commit suicide was because existence was unbearable even for him. And since the entire universe is essentially God's rotting corpse, there exists inside everything a will-to-die. Everything is doomed and destined to perish. And in a sense, this is true—the destiny of the universe, after all, is to expand and expand until it finally becomes cold and dead. Like a corpse.

Of all the philosophical pessimists, the most sympathetic to me was Peter Wessel Zapffe. According to him, the main problem with humanity is that we have too much consciousness. Unlike other animals, existence alone is not enough for us. We need a *reason* to exist. And that is why we have created endless different "reasons," one more arbitrary than the other. The problem, however, is that all of these reasons are ultimately make believe. The real universe is completely meaningless in every corner and exists without any purpose. Man has simply been the victim of an evolutionary error—he needs meaning in a universe which has none. And that is the tragedy of his existence.

According to Zapffe, humanity has invented four strategies to deal with this existential dilemma. The first strategy is to isolate all the unpleasant thoughts from our head and to banish them from our daily life. This is why most people love optimism and positive thinking, and why they don't want to dive existentially too deep for fear of what they might find.

Unfortunately, it is a strategy that is impossible for me. I have been preoccupied with the biggest philosophical questions ever since I was a teenager. I am also used to being honest with myself and have always pursued the truth to the point where it takes me, no matter how unpleasant the latter may be.

The second strategy is to anchor ourselves in artificial social institutions, such as the church, the state, and the family, and thus to live in the illusion of security that they offer. This is why people think family is the most important thing, why they go to war for their country, and why they go crazy to believe in an impossible god.

This is another strategy that does not work for me. Obviously, I don't believe in God; I'm amazed that anyone can at this point. As for country, beyond what practical possibilities it offers you, it is merely a historical idea that is meaningful only if you are brainwashed into thinking it is meaningful; in reality, there is only one planet, arbitrarily divided, its different cultures occupied with their own specific superstitions and delusions. And as far as the family is concerned, this is just another human idea; that a so-called bloodline connects you with someone in some way and that this connection is somehow significant is just an illusion. You owe nothing to your family except, of course, the "gift" you didn't ask for—your life.

The third strategy is to divert our thoughts with various meaningless pastimes, such as sports, alcohol, dancing, singing, violin practice, movies, TV, concerts, pornography, theater, weddings, parties, museums, swimming, skiing, celebrating Christmas, going to the zoo, buying technical gadgets, anime, video games and so on and so forth ad nauseam.

This doesn't work for me either. I have already tried all kinds of pastimes and entertainment to make my life more bearable. I've seen thousands of movies, read hundreds of books, and played plenty of brainless video games. I have traveled, not much, but enough to realize that all places are essentially the same underneath their facade. I have visited bars and restaurants, concerts and festivals, I've been on hikes and road trips. I've drank and I've fucked. But it's all too little in the end. Entertainment alone is not a sufficient reason to survive. Sooner or later, it starts to repeat itself. Sooner or later, it becomes boring and meaningless. Sooner or later, it makes me feel like just another mindless consumer, mindlessly consuming some worthless fucking product.

The fourth strategy is to sublimate the horrors of existence and use them to create some meaningful experience, such as a novel, a painting, a song, or even a philosophy—the latter of which Zapffe himself did. This is clearly the best of the four strategies. It might even theoretically work for me. Unfortunately, this is also the most difficult of the four strategies. Especially in a world where we are expected to slave our lives away at mindless jobs instead of creating art.

Although it was initially good to find such philosophical outcasts who had similar feelings about life as I did, this eventually grew into a testament on how goddamn bad life really is in this world and what a curse it is to be born. Philosophical pessimism thus made me feel more and more depressed. Unfortunately, it was too late to return to the land of naive dreams and happy fantasies—delusions in which the vast majority of humanity labored.

At the same time as my understanding of the world took root, there were, of course, also jobs and girlfriends. The jobs I was able to get without a higher education quickly became boring and unbearable. The girlfriends came and went without any of them ever being able to understand and accept me and my views.

Finally, due to the constant disappointments from school, family, philosophy, science, girlfriends, jobs, and existence in general, I began to drink. For drinking often made me forget the shittiness of everything even as it sometimes made me act erratically. The culmination of the latter was perhaps when I woke up after a night of heavy drinking in another city, my phone smashed, my money gone, my hands bloody. Although I didn't remember the last ten hours, all the signs pointed towards violence and insanity.

Of course, I knew deep down what had happened. When I drank enough alcohol whilst depressed—which I usually was—the anger over having been forced into this wretched world and having lived such an unsatisfactory life came bubbling out of me and finally exploded like dynamite. Alcohol removed the chains holding in check my wish for revenge over having to conform to the stupidity of everyday life. Alcohol turned Jekyll into Hyde. But Jekyll was only a facade. Hyde was there all along. Hyde was hatred for the world. And Jekyll the attempt to hide it.

And yet, there was something "positive" about the experience since I wrote a short story about it. It was the first story I wrote that was based entirely on my own life. And although I didn't realize it at the time, it could be considered a Zapffean attempt at sublimation—that is, I took my pain and created a work of art out of it. Unfortunately, every magazine I sent the story to refused to publish it.

I kept writing more short stories, but no one wanted to publish those either. It didn't help matters much that I didn't have any friends or acquaintances involved in writing or publishing. Because it was often through connections that people got things done in this corrupt society. Of course, it was also possible that the stories just sucked.

Nevertheless, I continued writing. Some of what I wrote was pure fiction whilst some was based on my own life. Obviously, due my worldview, everything I wrote tended to be pessimistic. And whether it was good or bad, it seemed unlikely that anyone would want to publish it because the stories focused mostly on negative things and didn't have happy endings.

Most people don't like gloomy and depressing stories, or even if they do, they need to have a happy ending. In horror fiction, the serial killer has to get caught, the monster has to die, the ghost has to be banished. A happy ending is expected. No matter how much suffering was caused, all's good that ends well. But what if the monster is reality itself? What if there can be no happy ending because the horror in the story comes from existence itself, which always ends in misery and disappointment? Who'd want to read that?

Out of all the stories I wrote—not that there were many because I was a perfectionist who lacked motivation—only one of them got published. It was one of the best feelings of my life. Even if it was just some obscure online magazine that didn't even pay me anything for it.

Inspired by this small success, I continued writing and sending stories to magazines. But none of them were accepted, and it usually took months to even get a rejection. One popular magazine managed to take an entire fucking year before they sent me a rejection. And so, the illusions around my writing career began to slowly crumble.

I tried to find other things to do in life. I tried exercising, traveling, other jobs, other girlfriends. But it was not enough. None of this was enough to make me content with life. Sooner or later, that same old thought crept back into my head—about how utterly futile everything is. How nothing is ultimately worth the bother. How it would have been better never to have been. And so, whenever I tried to find something in life worth doing, I soon lost interest in it. The only companion that never left me was my depression. Even as everyone else did.

Sometimes my depression turned into anger. Anger over not having any friends because I couldn't relate to people. Anger over my family not caring about what I was going through. Anger over the fact that I couldn't keep a relationship. And, above all, that I was born into this wretched world without a choice. My brain seemed to remember only the bad things and repeated them like a broken record. "See how bad your life is?" it constantly reminded me. "See how everything always keeps getting fucked? See how you're never happy with anything?"

"At least you're alive." That's what normal people say. As if it was such a blessing just to be alive. "You're making yourself unhappy with such thoughts." That's what my mother once told me. As though I was *deliberately* trying to make myself unhappy. People who say such things do not understand how the mind works. The mind is not a thing that exists in itself and that can be controlled; the mind is an illusion that arises from having thoughts. But what are thoughts? Thoughts are based on experience and information that's stored in the brain, which is activated when specific neurons become active in specific patterns. And since thoughts are made up of the co-activation of millions of such neurons, none of them separately form a thought, but only when many of them are activated at once does the "image" of a thought form in our heads.

As an analogy, one bit in a computer contains virtually no information, whereas many bits together can create an image on a computer screen. However, unlike the information on a computer hard drive, the images in our mind are much more vague and volatile and subject to change.

But where do these thoughts come from? Why do they occur in our brains? Is it because we choose to remember them? Do we choose to think about miserable things? Obviously not. Remembrance is a reaction—light enters our eyes or sound enters our ears, generating an electrical signal in the brain that travels to a certain area and causes synapses between certain neurons to exchange certain amounts of neurotransmitters; the pattern thus formed forms an image in our consciousness according to which we either automatically behave or not, depending on a number of circumstances.

The more we respond to the external stimuli that activate these patterns in our brain—which start out as very simple and become more complex over time, as is obvious when we consider the development of a child—the more we reinforce a particular thought and the more likely we are to remember it again the next time we react to the same things in our environment that are related to that thought.

Consciousness, on the other hand, is being aware that all this is happening. And while we mistakenly think that thoughts and decisions occur because *we* make them occur, the whole process is actually automatic. As Schopenhauer put it, we can do what we want, but we cannot want what we want.

Which brings me to free will. No matter what most people think, there is no freedom in anyone's choices in this world. Life is like a movie, and because we are aware of it, we think we could have changed the narrative if we had done something differently. But this "choice" is only an illusion. Studies have shown that the conscious idea that we could have done differently comes after the brain has already made the decision.

And because thoughts are automatic reactions that arise from physically encoded memories in our brains, our reactions to our environment are forced. The illusion of free will arose only because both people and their environments are complex and diverse, both with an unimaginable number of variables, all of which affect each other, which in turn affect each other, and so on until the end result becomes utterly unpredictable. But unpredictability is not the same as having free will.

Since we cannot see the specific sequence of events leading, like a mathematical calculation, to a specific "choice," we think that *we* made the choice, as if by magic, as if it was not influenced by anything other than our free will, which strangely is not affected by anything, not even the laws of nature. But choices are *always* influenced by something.

So where did our choices come from? From our environment. The environment created and shaped people at the same time as people created and shaped the environment. And if one of them is wretched, the other is likewise—a vicious circle from which there is no escape. But before people there was the environment. And since man has no free will to explain for his wickedness, the environment itself must be wicked. Which means that man is little more than a suffering puppet in a hostile universe.

At least that's how it looks when we anthropomorphize it. To be more objective, the universe does not even care enough about man to torture him, because it exists without any purpose. Humans are just the unhappy fragments of it that have become conscious. And most of these fragments are so weak and delirious that they accept every optimistic delusion they find and push it on others to make their short period of consciousness seem less empty, meaningless, and arduous than it really is.

Not only is our consciousness an illusion, as well as our "self" and free will, but in fact *everything* is an illusion if you think about it enough. Colors only exist when light bounces off objects and enters into our eyes. Even shapes are abstractions because nothing really touches other things; the perception of touch is an illusion created by electromagnetism. Not to mention that 99.9999999999999 percent of an atom—which make up all that we see—is empty space. The real universe is dark and without form, and we are only grouped parts of it that move about deterministically, all the while hallucinating a dream we call reality.

So if life is little more than an absurd dream, killing yourself is freeing yourself from it. And what does freedom look like? It looks like nothing. Because the only real freedom that exists is non-existence. There are always rules, conditions, and limitations for things that exist. There are no rules for things that do not exist; they are infinitely free, free not to be. Perhaps nothingness is our true home, as Cioran said, and existence is our exile? And perhaps entropy—like Mainländer's God who committed suicide—shows that the universe yearns for non-existence. Is *meant* for it. Because *that* is the natural state of things and not this aberration we call reality.

Entropy is said to measure the disorder of a system. But disorder is just a human concept. In truth, entropy only measures the heat loss of atoms, the inevitability of which is built into the laws of nature. This means that the universe is getting colder and colder until finally all the atoms in it have no heat and therefore no energy and therefore no movement. Which is when the so-called heat death of the universe occurs. Although atoms will still exist, because they no longer move, they do not come together and therefore there are no more molecules, and therefore no structures. In other words, because there are no more structures and movement, time ceases to exist.

Metaphorically: God shattered himself into a universe, but since God is immortal, his corpse will never completely decay. The only thing that happens to it is that its energy gets distributed over such a large area that even the smallest forms of energy are separated from each other. And since we are part of this corpse, we will not die either, only the illusion of our lives will.

It is said that when entropy in the universe has reached its maximum, there is a maximum amount of disorder. But let's think about this a little. Before human existence, is there less disorder or more? Is a person's life more characterized by order or disorder? It is *clearly* the latter. Disorder only changes into order when a person dies. And the same applies to the whole universe.

Before the universe, there was order. After the creation of the universe, there was disorder. From this disorder, structures such as stars and people were formed, both of them full of disorder. And when everything is finally broken down. When everyone is dead. When everything is gone. When everything reaches a non-existent state, a maximum state of order is finally achieved, not disorder. Because what is disorder? Well—look around you.

Popularizers of science keep saying how wonderful the universe is and how we are all connected in it because our bodies contain elements that came from exploding stars. There's even the saying, "We are the universe experiencing itself." But if that's true, isn't every suicide then the universe killing itself? As well as every murder, catastrophe, genocide, pandemic, war, and so on. In fact, isn't *all* the bad that has ever been done, then, the universe hurting itself? So what good are such meaningless and prosaic one-sided statements? They mean absolutely nothing.

And does it change the fact that we are forced into this world without a choice? A world where from an early age we are fed fabulous lies about how wonderful everything is and how everything is possible. But if all these fantastic things are possible, then why do they never materialize? Why do people end up working at McDonald's? Why do they inject heroin into their veins? Why do they lie? Why do they steal? Why do they rape? Why do they molest their children? Why do they kill themselves? Why do they kill others? Why do they keep torturing each other? For some reason, our parents never mention these things. Or if they do, they blame it on the person themselves. How fucking convenient!

And when someone gets depressed because they have to live in this fraudulent society—again, without a choice—they are declared mentally ill and brainwashed by drugs or therapy. That's *really* convenient. It's always easier to blame the victim. When in reality, this whole fucking world is one big insane asylum, and feeling depressed about having been forced into it is the most natural reaction in the whole world.

And when someone kills themselves, we're shocked. But why? They merely stood up against the scam they were born into. The scam called life—a giant pyramid scheme in which the victims keep creating more and more victims. It is said that life is a gift. But we have not asked for this gift, it has been forced upon us. And secondly, the gift stinks.

And since euthanasia is not legal in our primitive world—interesting how we are forced into it but not allowed to leave—then suicide is the only way to escape from this hell. Killing yourself is, after all, just the disruption of the mechanisms that create consciousness and keep the body alive. By putting a bullet in my head, I am simply speeding up a life that is going to end in death anyway. The question is, when? And how much suffering do I have to go through before I've had enough?

Nietzsche said that to live is to suffer and to survive is to find some meaning in the suffering. But what if there is no meaning, only illusions? And what if those illusions have all stopped working, as they have for me?

Well, in such case, there's only *one* solution left—the one you can see before you.

PS: Excuse all the blood.

It was three in the morning and the bottle of whiskey was half empty when I finally finished writing. I was reminded of a joke by George Carlin in which a writer tries to write a suicide note, but keeps making more and more drafts of it, ending up with a book proposal instead which gives him a reason to live. Yet though I was used to making many drafts of my stories, I decided to leave this as my first and final draft, no matter what Hemingway said. Besides, Hemingway was dead. By his own hand.

I grabbed the whiskey bottle and took a big hit from it. I let my drunken eyes wander across the room. They came to a stop at the cartridge inside the shot glass, and my thoughts turned towards entropy again. More specifically, on my reinterpretation of it.

Order and disorder. Before I existed, there was order. After I was born, there was disorder. The longer I lived, the more disorder there was. And right now, there was more disorder than there had ever been. My mind was fucked up. As was my life. And it was only with my death that there would be order again. At least for me.

But what had made it into such a disordered state? Well, it had been many things. But mainly it had been one thing. A person. A person called Vicky. Yeah, I know, she had no choice in the end. But neither did I for resenting her for it.

I continued drinking the whiskey.

35

I WOKE UP TO the sound of a demonic female scream. It took me a while before I realized that it had only been a dream. I was laying on the living room floor with a throbbing headache. My right hand was covered with dried blood and the skin on my knuckles was broken.

I saw that the room had been trashed—the table lamp was shattered; framed pictures lay on the ground, their glass broken; alcohol bottles, drinking glasses, books, DVDs, candle holders, a wall clock, and all sorts of knick-knacks had been thrown all across the room. The cherry on top of the shit pie was a picture of Vicky attached to the wall with a black butterfly knife through her face. Disorder indeed. I had acted like Orson Welles at the end of Citizen Kane. And I didn't remember anything.

When I went into the bathroom to vomit, I saw that the mirror on the wall had been broken; it seemed by my fist. There was also a small table mirror that Vicky had left behind which had been thrown in the bathtub into a thousand pieces.

After I had finished vomiting out my insides, I looked into the broken mirror. A fragmented monster looked back. I had a black eye, my eyebrow was busted, there was a wound on my head, my hair was disheveled, my clothes were dirty, my face was anemic. I looked like I was half dead already. All I needed was to kill the other half.

I went looking for the gun I had received from the Russian. I wondered for a moment whether the whole incident could have only been a dream because of its inherent absurdity . . . until I found the gun laying on the living room floor. I picked it up and examined it. It was made out of metal, and it was heavy; it was, without a doubt, real. Looking at it, I recalled a passage from the end of *Will O' the Wisp*: "A revolver is solid, it is made of steel. It is an object. To come up against an object at last."

Apart from alcohol, this book—inspired from the author's friend who had committed suicide—had been my only companion for the past week. And now I was going to be inspired by it. It was life imitating art imitating life.

Of course, no book could actually cause anyone to commit suicide. At best, it could give you but a small push that could come from anywhere. In my case, it was no single thing that had led to this point but many things in tandem. The direction had been set many years ago—in fact since the beginning of the universe—and it was now time for the culmination. The finale. The wild finish.

In the end, it wasn't even my decision to kill myself.

Because I was only a small part of the universe. It was the universe, constantly at war with itself, constantly tearing at itself for no reason, that had randomly decided to remove another conscious part of it for no better reason than having tortured it enough. And that was all right by me. For I did not condemn the universe for it, because I was sure that the universe was just another victim of external circumstances, just like anyone who has suffered ill or done ill in this evil world of ours. Because in the end, not even the universe had a choice whether to exist or not. And if the universe was God's corpse, then I was sure that even God didn't have a choice whether or not to kill himself. He was simply forced to. Because the pain had become unbearable. As it had for me.

I took the cartridge from the shot glass and loaded it. With the gun in my hand, I sat down on the couch, considering where I should do it. For some reason, I didn't want to do it on the couch. I'd get blood on it; blood that would never come out. So I decided to do it on the floor instead. Yes, I know; it was absurd to care about the couch. But it was merely one absurd act in an absurd life. In other words, a sure-fire sign of being human, all too human.

I kneeled down on the floor, as if in front of God. But there was no God. There was no one to look out for this miserable soul who'd had enough of the vicissitudes of fate. There no one that cared for me. Not Vicky. Not my mom. Not my dad. Not a non-existent God. Not society. Not the universe. Not even me.

I pulled down the safety lever on the Makarov. All I had to do now was pull the trigger. It was such an easy thing to do that I wondered why more people didn't. Was it because they were against guns? I smiled at my last stupid joke, as tears started flowing down my face.

I tried to find some last-minute reason not to go through with it, but I couldn't find any. Besides, a million people committed suicide each year. It was nothing extraordinary. I wasn't special. Although it may have been a tragedy for me, for the world at large I was just another number.

I placed the gun barrel against the right side of my head, aiming it more or less so that the bullet would penetrate the center of my brain.

I inhaled in and out a few times, tears flowing down my face. "To die," I quoted to an invisible audience, "is the finest thing you could do, the most positive, the most you could do."

I closed my eyes and pulled the trigger.

Sublimation

THERE WAS A CLICK, but nothing happened. I pulled the trigger again. Click. Still nothing. I aimed the gun at the wall and pulled the trigger. Click. Nothing.

I lowered my arm and looked at the gun. What happened? Was it God? Had he intervened at the last minute because he cared? Did he stop me from killing myself?

I chuckled. Of course not. The gun had jammed. Guns did that from time to time. And although the probability of it happening was relatively small, unlike miracles, it *did* happen. Especially with old and poorly maintained guns, which this Makarov appeared to be. It wasn't divine intervention, only a coincidence. A coincidence that had been predestined since the beginning of the universe.

I sat back on the couch. Now what? I considered my options. I couldn't jump from high up because I was afraid of heights. Hanging myself didn't seem like such a good idea anymore; besides, I didn't have any rope. Shooting range? I'd rather not; the instructor was right next to you and might intervene, meaning I might end up in jail or an insane asylum instead. I couldn't cut my veins because I was afraid of pain. Nor did I have enough pills, which I couldn't take anyway because of the fear of pain. My situation reminded me of Dorothy Parker's poem *Résumé*.

I located my pack of cigarettes, took one, and lit it. I took a drag from the cigarette and observed the chaos in my apartment. It was amazing that no one had called the police. But then I remembered that I only had a month left to live there anyway.

I didn't know what I was going to do. There was no doubt that I had reached the lowest point in my entire life. I had read somewhere that when Nietzsche had reached a similarly low point, he had decided to become an optimist. How he had achieved that magic trick, I had no idea. The hole I had dug for myself seemed only fitting for a grave.

When I was finished with the cigarette, I lit a new one and looked out the window. Eventually, my thoughts went back to Zapffe and his existential coping strategies. More specifically, the fourth one. Sublimation. Using your pain to create art. Of turning muck into gold. Art, according to Nietzsche, was the proper task of life.

Although I didn't like most so-called art—especially pretentious modern art—what I liked I liked dearly, such as my favorite novels. I adored works that were sincere and authentic, that spoke of the suffering of their authors, of their misery and humiliation, of their despair, and, perhaps, also about their hope.

The books I was able to relate to—as rare as that

was—was something extraordinary for me. It was more valuable than anything else in the world. And so . . . what if I tried writing a book like that? About my suffering? About my disappointments? About my insights? After all, weren't most of my favorite books written in similarly shitty circumstances that I was in? Perhaps that's where their authenticity stemmed from? From rock bottom.

After all, it was almost impossible for a successful person to be authentic, because in order to be successful in our world, you had to be a pretender and have ten different masks for ten different people. And I only had one—my own face.

In theory, I had even already written one chapter. The suicide note. The book could be about all that had led up to it—this last dreadful week, which had been both tragic and meaningful. At least for me. And if it was meaningful to me, maybe it would be for others. Others that have felt themselves alienated from human society, not fit to live in the world and the world not fit for them to live in it.

Writing a book like that may not solve all of my problems. But it would at least give me the opportunity to use my pain to create something for a change, instead of only using it to destroy. And that alone may be enough to stay alive a little while longer. A book, according to Cioran, is a suicide postponed. And there was always the rest of my life to kill myself.

Whether the book would end up being considered

good or bad didn't matter. The only thing that mattered was that it was authentic. That it was honest. That it didn't hold back. That its contents, as Nietzsche put it, were written with the author's own blood.

And if you're reading this, then perhaps I've succeeded. And I hope you will too.

THE END

ABOUT THE AUTHOR

Keijo Kangur is an author from Estonia who has written poetry, film and video game reviews, historical and philosophical articles, short stories, a travelogue, and a novel. He writes in both Estonian and English.

Coming from a working-class background, he has worked as a telemarketer, in construction, at a warehouse, at a pizza parlor, as a postal sorter, at call centers, as a data entry clerk, for an airline, and as an anti-money laundering investigator.

Although he has never been to college, he has spent years studying philosophy, science, and literature. From his studies and life experience he has developed views which may be compared to those expressed by Rust Cohle in the TV series True Detective. Above all, he considers himself an antinatalist.

His favorite fiction is the kind that is based on the author's own life and focuses on the darker side of existence. His own works likewise draw strongly from his real-life experiences and revolve around the darker aspects of being.

Despite all this, he *does* possess a sense of humor and tries not to take himself too seriously all the time.

Please consider leaving a review on Amazon or Goodreads.

Thank you.

Printed in Great Britain
by Amazon